# A Dark Night, A Long Night

By Trevor Lewis

Copyrighted to Trevor Lewis, Dunedin, New Zealand August 2011

First Published August 2011

ISBN    978-0-473-19332-4

# Preface

'**A Dark Night, A Long Night**' gives a Sci Fi genre answer to a question that many of us ask from time to time. That question being, 'What if?' In this case, what if those who are in power are wrong? What if the exact opposite of what we are told is happening is in fact occurring much to our unpreparedness?

The story also looks at possible repercussions that scientists, and those of us with a serious interest in science sometimes face when experimenting with what we don't really fully understand. In 'A Dark Night, A Long Night' the repercussions are life changing, and in fact World changing.

The city referred to in this book as Duntoon, is loosely based on a wonderful city full of historical significance called Dunedin, located around three quarters of the way down the East Coast of the South Island of New Zealand. Dunedin is the home to the University of Otago, arguably the top University in New Zealand, which is also noted as having the only dental school in New Zealand, which many overseas students attend. Dunedin also has within its boundaries the only accessible Albatross colony in the World, New Zealand's only castle, the World's steepest street, the only fully covered in grass surface stadium in the World, a huge Cadbury Chocolate factory (including Cadbury World), and numerous other nature based attractions. Add to all of this the dozens of quality restaurants and bars; Dunedin is a top location that should be on every visitor's list of places to visit while in New Zealand.

I hope you will enjoy this story as much as I enjoyed writing it, and will follow the story further in the books that will follow this one, and expand on the happenings in and around the fictional city called Duntoon in the non-fictional and beautiful country of New Zealand.

Lastly, thanks to my beautiful Wife Di, and wonderful children Richard, Emma, Samuel, and Katherine for putting up with me yet again as I struggled to get another book finished. Also thanks to the many fans that followed the story online in it's draft stages, and then persevered for many months waiting for the full story via this hard copy to be finished.

**Trevor Lewis**

*This book is dedicated to those who fight to uphold a rare attribute these days – something called common sense.*

*Join the Facebook group – 'A Dark Night, A Long Night' to keep up with new books in this saga to be released in coming months*

# A Dark Night, A Long Night

**By Trevor Lewis**

## CHAPTER ONE

**The storm hadn't been that bad**, or that unusual, though it is fair to say it left an impression on many in the city. This impression was due to the storm not being forecast by the meteorological service, often referred to by Adam as the 'guessing with fingers crossed service'.

Adam had been at work on his security patrol of Duntoon University the night of the storm, and though loving the lightning and thunder as he always did, he cursed the downpour as he hadn't packed his long oilskin coat, and ended up getting drenched. He was an imposing figure at 6 feet 4 inches, and muscular with it. Yet his gentle though well defined face overcame the imposing nature of his stature and immediately put people at rest, and assured them he meant no harm.

Tricia wasn't working the night of the storm, as it was her night off from her Emergency Department nurse's position at the hospital. However, unlike her husband Adam, she didn't enjoy the lightning or thunder, but did enjoy hearing the rain landing on the tin roof of their small yet well maintained and tidy cottage. She wasn't a stunning looking woman, yet every guy or girl who she came across immediately fell in love with her sparkling blue eyes, and her charming smile.

"I loved hearing each rain drop hit the roof" Tricia told Adam the next morning after he arrived back home, "It was like hearing a hundred tiny heartbeats all beating, not in unison, but all for the same purpose and all striving to be heard".

"Oh Tricia, for such a pretty lady, and wonderful Wife, you talk such utter rubbish sometimes " Adam laughed.

"Why thank you my loving husband!" she replied as she gently nudged him in the ribs.

"I thought it was supposed to be fine last night though, I wouldn't have left the washing on the line if I had known it was going to pour down! You can never trust the weather in Duntoon."

"Tell me about it, my uniform is like a wet sponge. I had to change into my civi's before I even finished my shift. Oh, and hey, don't blame good old Duntoon, blame that frigging guessing with fingers crossed service! They think they can forecast what will happen in a hundred years time, when they cant even get the next twelve hours right!"

The city of Duntoon wasn't a small city, not by New Zealand standards anyway, with around 100,000 permanent residents plus over 22,000 students during the tertiary year. The city was spread over an area of over 3300 square kilometres, making it one of the biggest cities in the World by land area. However most of that land was rural, with the populated city area itself only taking up a small percentage.

Perhaps the most notable feature of Duntoon, at least to those who lived elsewhere in the Country, was Duntoon University. Duntoon truly fitted the label of being a "University City", as the main City area was virtually built around the many University buildings, big and small. Several of those buildings were intermingled among the business and apartment buildings, as well as the large University Campus highlighting the tertiary focus of the city.

Jack and Susan had lived in Duntoon all their lives, as had their Parents. They were sister and brother, and both choosing to live lives of semi-solitude had decided to share a house in their advancing years, to save on costs and loneliness. Jack being 61, and Susan 63, they weren't exactly old codgers as yet, but Jack certainly complained like one, according to Susan. The high-jinx activities of the students of Duntoon University were one of Jack's favorite issues to complain about, in addition to the usual conversational topics of the older generation such as the Government, local Council, and of course the weather.

"Jack, of course the lawn is soaked, it rained heavily last night for goodness sake!"

"I know Susan, I'm not stupid. But how am I supposed to cut the damn lawn if it's like Lake Taupo out there!" Jack mumbled back as he walked out the front door, red band gumboots on, splashing with each step if more for dramatic effect than from the result of excess rainfall.

Susan laughed to herself and smiled, she loved her brother and despite his ability to rub anyone up the wrong way within a minute of meeting them, she knew his heart was as soft as a feather when it came to caring for and helping others. This gave Jack the ability to bring people to all but wringing his neck when they first met him, to wanting to be his lifelong friend within a couple of hours of knowing him.

As Jack continued down the long drive on their semi rural property, he noticed something, well, something that could only be described by Jack as "Damn odd!" Their property was the furthermost of residential dwellings before you left the semirural city area, and they had a fairly good view of the tar-seal highway winding itself through the hills and making its way towards the North. The 'damn odd' thing that Jack noticed was a cloud of dust, or possibly smoke – or maybe both, sitting over the furthest stretch of the highway, just beyond clear visibility.

"What the heck" Jack said to himself," you'd think someone was digging up the damn highway, with all that dust, or is that a bush fire?"

# CHAPTER TWO

Tricia packed the last of the bags into the station wagon. Though the wagon was Adam's pride and joy, his "Baby", Adam like most males had no skill in packing up a vehicle for the holidays. Though they were only going away for three nights, and only traveling just on 100kms, Tricia had packed enough supplies for at least a week.

"Trish, are you sure you have left room for the kitchen sink, it's about the only thing you haven't packed in there," Adam joked.

"Well, you never can have enough clothes or food, especially at the rate you go through both. Now hurry up and lock the house up so we can get going young man." Tricia winked at Adam, knowing he loved the fact he was three years younger than her, and continually reminded her accordingly.

Within a few minutes, Tricia and Adam were in the 'big green monster', which is what Trish preferred to call the wagon, much to Adam's disgust.

"It is NOT a monster; it's my baby, baby."

The 1972 Ford Galaxie 500 was originally Adam's Dad's car, purchased almost new in late 1973. Despite many repairs, and many unplanned hold ups at the side of the highway waiting for tow trucks over the years, the wagon was his Dad's pride and joy, and Adam continued the love and care it had always been given. New Zealanders often had love affairs with their cars, and although some would describe the relationship between Adam and his vehicle in that way, Tricia by far took precedence in his love life.

As they drove onto the highway heading North, Tricia picked up her mobile to call her Parents, who were already at the campground they were heading for. Adam's Parents had both passed away some years ago, his Dad passing away three years ago, two years after his Mother died from a blood disorder. Adam had become quite close to Tricia's Parent's, and they accepted him as part of their family, as if he always had been.

"Strange, no signal. The network must be offline AGAIN! Pass me your mobile Adam, I'll try yours."

Tricia dialed the number again from Adam's work mobile, which was connected to a different network provider; yet again there was no signal.

"We usually get good coverage all round here," Adam said, puzzled about what the problem could be. "Turn the radio on, its nearly news time, see if we can find out if the network is out just in this area, or whether it is nationwide".

"What the heck? I can't get any of the main stations, but I found a local one."

"News on 454 FM," the speaker blasted out, with the stereotypical news music playing in the background. "Headlines at twelve. All radio and telephone connections between Duntoon and the rest of the country have been cut. Duntoon Police search for the cause of all traffic coming into the city having stopped since around 5am this morning ..." the news continued, with Tricia and Adam looking at each other, not quite knowing what to say or think.

"What's this all about Adam? Do you think that storm last night brought down lines or something?" Tricia asked.

"Looks like it. I would say that is probably what has blocked the highways as well, you know, lines down, maybe ruptured storm water drains, that kind of thing."

"Yeah I guess so. I didn't think the storm was that bad though? Hey, it's weird but kind of cool driving along the highway with no traffic coming the other way," Tricia laughed, if only half heartedly. "But I suppose this also means we might not be able to get to the campground then?"

"Oh, I think by the time we reach wherever the problem is, they will have the roads cleared by then. Can't be too far though, otherwise we would still have traffic from Oldstown getting through, that's the nearest town to the north of us. The highway blockage must be between us and them."

# CHAPTER THREE

The highway that took the many tourists and locals from Duntoon through to Oldstown, a quaint reasonably large town around 100 kilometres north of the city, was a pleasure to drive on. The scenery was breathtaking in places, ranging from ocean views to rolling green hills that were often partially snow covered in mid to late winter. Fur seal colonies, along with places to sometimes catch penguins making their way ashore in the evenings were tourist highlights. The highway itself was in pretty good shape, being part of the number one highway for New Zealand, linking one end of the Country to the other.

Adam and Tricia continued their drive, discussing where the damage to the highway must be. As they drove around one of the most sweeping corners in the highway, the road came to an end. In fact, there was literally no tar-seal road there at all.

With Tricia screaming, Adam quickly braked hard and swerved, but not quickly enough. The huge Ford Galaxy skidded from the remaining tar-sealed highway off of an approximate half meter drop to clay, dirt, long overgrown grass, and narrowly missing a cluster of small and medium size bushes and a large tree. They eventually came to a halt in a cloud of dust, with clumps of dirt being thrown into the air.

"Adam, are you ok? What the hell is going on?" Tricia trembled as she spoke.

Not just had the highway come to a sudden and traumatic end from the corner, there was no more highway to be seen. Instead there was grass, shrubs, trees, and heavy bush, like no highway had ever existed past this point.

"I have no idea Trish, but whatever is going on, it's blowing my mind I'll tell you that, this is just too much babe, just too much!"

The big green monster sat where it had landed, with Adam and Tricia still sitting in it several minutes after they landed where they wondered if this was to become the Monster's final resting place. Staring, shaking their heads, trying to speak, but not quite knowing what to say, they felt bewilded. Their World had changed inexplicably and unexpectedly.

Having what you know and accept ripped from your mind, and replaced with something that isn't logical, is something that stops people in their tracks. We are not designed for, nor accepting of such sudden and dramatic change, and when it occurs, we flounder and wonder what to do, or whether in fact we can do anything at all. In the depths of every person's heart is a need for some type of routine, achievable expectations, and having control and knowledge of what is occurring around us. Maybe this is why there is such unrest in society today, as technology advances on almost by the day, we are left behind in a constant state of feeling like we are losing control of what we knew was so, just the day before. This sentiment was certainly accurate for the situation that Adam and Tricia now found themselves in.

"You sure you are ok Trish?"

"Yeah, yeah I'm fine. My neck hurts a little, but yeah - I'm ok, honest."

"Let's see if we can get out of this wreck."

"Wreck Adam? I thought this was your baby?" Tricia jived, trying to somehow refocus his mind, and hers, on the way things were, smiles and jokes and love, before what they knew disappeared as they flew through the air and off of the highway.

"No, not any more, now it's just a wreck. Just a wreck. Let's get out of here, and see if we can make sense of all this crap."

Both Tricia and Adam found that the doors still opened, and they climbed out of the wagon, into the long grass that awaited them. They looked around, walked about in the calf high seemingly untouched grass, listened, and even smelt the air as if somehow it might reveal some answers. The wagon had burst two tyres, and looked like it had broken its entire suspension when it hit the ground. The big green monster had been fatally injured.

"Look at this Trish, what the heck has happened to it?" Adam had walked some 10 meters back to the edge of the highway that still existed, and gestured to the edge that led down to the land that appeared to never have had tarmac on it.

"It looks as though something red hot has sliced it, and taken away the highway that used to be right where we are standing, and left the rest of it untouched. I mean, look at it Trish, the edge of the tar seal has almost a mirror finish to it, its not crumbled, no signs of any bits broken off it, just cut, and gone." The volume of Adam's voice lowered so it was barely audible for the last few words. He was literally lost for words, or at least for a rational explanation.

"It's just plain weird, maybe, um; maybe the lightning hit it or something? Or, I know Adam, ha-ha its simple! We must have somehow driven down a side road, this isn't the highway at all. Maybe it's an old highway, which was never finished! Oh man are we dumb!" Tricia began to laugh, though after looking up and along the highway, she stopped suddenly as she realised Adam had focused on something as she was speaking, and now she focused on the same thing. A red highway sign with the number one on it. There was no doubt this was the main highway, or at least was until it reached the point where they now stood.

As Adam was about to speak a Police car sped around the same bend they had traveled along just minutes before, but unlike Adam the cop didn't brake quick enough, and the speed he left the highway was maybe twice as fast as they had in the wagon. The patrol car went bonnet first into the dirt, flipping three to four times, end over end, taking out a clump of scrub before coming to rest on its roof.

"Oh no!" Tricia screamed, "Adam, is he ok?"

Adam rushed to the patrol car, sitting some 30 meters away now, laying near a large redwood tree. Looking in through the drivers door window, he saw the officer was conscious, but barely so. He looked at Adam out through the now shattered windscreen.

"Craziness, its everywhere," the middle aged officer muttered, though Adam wasn't sure whether he was talking to himself, or to him.

"Are you ok man?" Adam asked.

"The highway, just stopped, it just frigging stopped!" The officer replied. "What is going on in this city? Down south and out west they are reporting the same thing. The highway just stops, like it was never there. I thought it was a practical joke, like you know, I was being set up!"

"Trish, it's everywhere babe, we are isolated," Adam called out to Trish who was approaching slowly, knowing she should administer first aid as she was trained to do, yet afraid of what she might see inside the smashed up vehicle.

"It's not just the highways," the officer paused, choking on blood that now slowly trickled from his mouth. "On the Western highway, Sergeant Johnson said where the highway ended so did a house that was there. It was now just half a house, the rest just replaced with bush, no sign of any debris from the rest of the house, it just, it just didn't exist anymore." He choked on his blood again, and fell unconscious.

Adam looked up and over at Tricia.

"It's ok Adam, I heard. I want Mum, I need her, I want my Mum, now!"
She began to cry, uncontrollably.

# CHAPTER FOUR

After he had made sure the Police Officer had a clear airway, or as clear as Adam could make it in the circumstances, he walked over to Tricia, put his arm around her and just stood silently, being there but knowing words couldn't comfort someone who yearned for the Parent they loved, yet who was now beyond their reach for how long – no one knew.

Each and every one of us face a time where feeling alone hits us in a way that tears our heart open, and even though we may be surrounded by people, even other loved ones, that feeling of loneliness and need doesn't abate. That feeling is sometimes brought on by the loss of someone very special, but other times it is just being so far away from them that the void is unbearable.

Once Tricia's tears stopped flowing, and her body ceased to tremble, Adam held her hand and led her towards the Patrol car.

"You need to use your skills and knowledge Trish. He needs you, until we get some more help here. Do what you do well honey, it will help you refocus from what's going on." Adam smiled at Trish, and eventually she smiled back at him and nodded.

"I need to do something to warn other drivers," he told her "and we need to somehow get some transport here to get this guy to the hospital."

Just as Adam reached the edge of the highway that still was, yet still stood on the highway that was no longer, both he, and Trish who was now at the side of the patrol car, heard another vehicle approaching.

"Oh no, not again Adam, no, stop him Adam, stop him before he crashes too!" Tricia screamed at Adam.

But before Adam could even jump up onto where the tarmac began, a small truck rounded the corner. However, the truck was traveling relatively slowly, and after braking heavily, it stopped before it too tumbled from the edge of the highway, 'the edge of reality' Adam thought to himself.

A large Maori man, maybe in his sixties, hopped out of the driver's side, and a very cute blonde woman, aged in her 30's, jumped out from the passenger seat.

"Blimen heck mate, what's going on here?" the man, who it turned out went by the name of Henry, called out.

"You tell us," Adam replied. "But one thing's for sure, we need you to get back to town or the nearest house and see if you can get an ambulance and fire crew out here. There's no way I can get the cop out of his car, he's still breathing, but he needs help bad."

"Mate, we can radio back and get Sally to get onto the Ambo's," Henry replied. "Di, get on the RT sweetie, and get someone out here now."

"Um, firstly, please don't all me sweetie, Henry, and secondly I have an advanced first aid certificate, and I have already grabbed the First Aid kit so get your ass into the truck and radio back." With that, Di jumped onto the grass, and ran to the patrol car, joining Tricia, and after a hurried introduction to each other they did what they could for the boy in blue.

"Henry, there's no signal man. We can't get any signal on our phones," Adam said.

"Well, the RT back to Duntoon HQ works fine mate. But when I tried to get the yard in Oldstown, nothing." Henry shook his head.

Around twenty-five minutes later, an Ambulance had arrived, as had a fire engine. Henry had parked his truck 100 metres back on a straight stretch of highway, with the yellow beacon lights flashing, and some road cones out to warn others to stop, and turn back. Henry and Di had been sent out to what the council believed must be a highway blocked with tree's down or a landslide. They were to find the blockage, cone it off for safety and report back about what machinery was needed. As it turned out, it wasn't a highway blockage they needed to cone off, but rather the end of the road, literally.

The ambulance soon left with the badly injured officer, but the fire crew hung around for a few minutes longer, looking, wondering, as mystified as was Adam, Tricia, Henry and Di. Others travelling on the highway were saved from having their minds messed with by the sight, as they were turned back before they could see what lay ahead.

Eventually the fire crew left, heading back to their chief, and wondering how they would explain the unexplainable to him.

"Adam, come on, get in the truck with Henry and me, he's heading back in, they have coned off the highway and two police patrols are on their way to close it properly. Di is going to stay here until they get here, make sure no idiots ignore the cones," Tricia said, looking a little more accepting of the mystery they had found themselves embroiled in, involuntarily, but desperate to have Adam join her in their escape back to the city where hopefully some normality remained.

Adam stood by his now deceased big green monster, "the wreck" and looked about, almost oblivious to what Tricia had just said.

"You go, I can't, not now," Adam eventually replied.

"Adam! Don't be stupid; get in this truck right now! Don't you do this to me!" Tricia shouted back.

Adam was a lover of his big Green Monster, of Tricia, and also a lover of mysteries that needed solving. He would often spend dozens of hours pondering over unsolved crimes detailed in the media, coming up with his own hypotheses of what may have happened to the unfortunate victim. Trish didn't usually hold him back from this hobby of his, maybe because it seemed more of a need than a hobby, but this time she needed him with her, and not wandering around a paddock of intrigue at the end of a highway now seemingly heading to nowhere.

"It's alright love," Henry said to her, "I'll be back later to get Di, just give him some time, he needs to get his head around this, like we all do. Di will keep an eye on him, won't ya sweetie, uh, I mean Di?" Henry winked at Trish, trying to put a smile on her face.

"Yes, don't you worry Trish, I'll keep an eye on him, make sure he doesn't get himself into any trouble." Di smiled the kind of smile that sent out warmth, sincerity and what can only be described as genuine affection. She was one of the few people we may meet in a lifetime who are what you see and hear from them, they live what they say and what they believe, and this was evident in Di's eyes, and in her smile.

"Thank you Di. He's a good man, but he is so damn stubborn, and he loves a mystery, and somehow I doubt he will ever come across a greater one than this, maybe no one ever will."

Tricia climbed out of the truck, walked over to Adam, hugged him, kissed him on the cheek, said nothing, but looked into his eyes for nearly a minute. She then walked back to the truck, sat close to Henry, and they drove off headed back towards Duntoon.

Adam watched the truck disappear into the distance, and then walked over to the redwood tree where the patrol car had come to rest earlier, and where the middle of the highway should have still been.

As he looked up to the top of the tree he muttered, "My God, this must be 20 years old, how the heck did this get here."

Di strolled over to him, also looking up at the magnificent tree.

"No, Adam, this tree is not 20 years old, I know a lot about trees, horticulture was my major at Duntoon University. This tree," Di sighed, and looked Adam directly in the eyes "this tree is at least 200 years old."

They stared at each other, they then stood staring at the tree in silence for what seemed an eternity, Adam shaking his head as if somehow denial would change what was, or at least what seemed to have become.

# CHAPTER FIVE

Jack and Susan's property wasn't extensive, but it was a lot bigger than the traditional quarter acre that historically most New Zealand residents used to yearn after. At around 6 acres there was enough room for Susan's pride and joy, her two horses. There was also enough acreage for Jack's rather odd obsession, goats. Jack had six goats. Bob, Ted, Sarah, George, Lucky, and Doozey.

Lucky was the last goat that Jack had added to the growing menagerie. His name came about from when Jack was loading Doozey onto his trailer at a farm some 10 kilometers from his home. The farm owner he was purchasing Doozey from had accidentally left his tractor's brake off, which subsequently rolled forward, straight towards another goat that Jack was not purchasing. This goat got such a fright it jumped several feet in the air, literally landing in Jack's trailer beside Doozey.

"Wow, damn it that was Lucky," Jack shouted, "Ha, well what the heck I'll take him too - Lucky, yeah ha-ha, Lucky."

Jack had wandered around the front lawn for nearly twenty minutes. He took great pride in cutting their lawn with his ride on mower, but on this morning rather than the lawn receiving a cut, it was the sole audience to Jack's muttering to himself about the "Damn rain, damn forecasters, and the damn lawn,"

Eventually Jack, and possibly the lawn, had had enough, and Jack walked back inside the house.

"Susan, I'm going to have to leave that lawn until it dries up. It's like a damn sponge!"

"Jack, you need to hear what's on the news, it's real strange."

"Strange? I'll tell you what's strange, why the heck the radio news has to talk about the damn weather, I already know it rained last night!"

"No Jack, it's not about the weather. They are saying something about Duntoon being cut off from the rest of the country, no way in or out, at least not by car anyway. They also say you can't call anyone outside of Duntoon on landline or mobile. I tried getting Betty and Eric in Oldstown, but it just gives a disconnected signal, "Tricia explained, with a worried tone to her voice.

"See, damn weather talk Susan, that's what I said! Storm has knocked out the phones, and blocked the highway, whoop de damn do! I'm going to get the truck out and drive up the highway and see if that useless council of ours has got off their backside and started to clear the road yet."

With that, Jack stormed off outside still mumbling.

"Damn council can't get a bit of dirt cleared from the highway; I'll show them what work is. Wasn't a civil engineer for nothing, useless bunch of old sods"

Jack jumped in his white 1970 Bedford truck, which was still in almost new condition, except the odd small dent and scratch, and headed onto the highway and towards Oldstown.

---------------------------------------------

Di heard the vehicle first. "That must be the police patrols, finally, it's been 40 minutes!"

Adam looked towards the highway, still standing in the calf high grass, still baffled by what he saw. But instead of a police patrol car rounding the bend, an old white Bedford truck came straight towards them.

Di and Adam frantically waved their arms at Jack, who braked and used his gears to slow the truck, which came to a stop just after its front wheels left the end of the tarsealed highway, and hit the awaiting mystery land.

"Damn it! What has that council stuffed up this time?" Jack shouted, "What the heck do they think they are doing diverting us off the highway, and up here? I could have killed myself!"

Jack didn't seem to understand he was in fact in the right place, yet that place was now something totally different from which it once was. Jack had come across the cones spread across the road, but being a "Civil Engineer" he wasn't going to let a few cones and a 'Road Closed' sign stop him from checking out the problem and getting it sorted.

"Why is that Police car upside down?" Jack queried. It quickly dawned on him what a silly question that was, and that he had also just fallen down the rabbit hole and joined Alice and the mad hatter in a game of "Reality replaced by a crazy dream" poker. But unfortunately in this game, there were no winners, and no one got to take the first turn, but instead they spent the entire time trying to decipher the rules.

"Why? What? Who - are you two?" Jack asked.

Di and Adam introduced themselves, and tried to tell Jack what they knew, he in turn told them what Susan had told him of the news on the radio.

"Oh, can you two tell me something?" Jack said, looking at Di "Why is it so damn cold?"

Adam and Di hadn't noticed until now, maybe because they had been in a constant state of shock, but the temperature was only around 10 degrees Celsius, yet it was the middle of summer. But when they all got up onto the tar-sealed highway, to look at how they would try and get the truck back up there, they felt the temperature rise higher the further they moved from where the tar seal now ended, to maybe around 22 degrees just thirty or so metres from the highway end, which is the average temperature that could be expected at that time of year.

"Well I'll be damned," said Jack.

# CHAPTER SIX

Henry rounded the corner to see Adam and Di had been joined by one other. He also saw that the number of incapacitated vehicles had grown by one. It was a beauty at that.

"Nice truck, that yours old Fella?" Henry asked Jack.

"Old fella? Ha-ha, you got to be older than me! But yeah, he's my truck alright, you wouldn't give an old fella like me a tow would you?" Jack replied

They soon had a rope from Henry's truck attached, and with some drama and numerous "Damns" from Jack, managed to get it back onto the highway.

"I thought there were supposed to be some Police patrols coming out here Henry?" Di asked.

"Yeah, well, according to the news there has been a couple of cops murdered out West, where the, well you know, where the highway ends."

"Murdered? What the heck?" Adam said.

"Yeah, apparently. So that's where all the cops are headed, to sort it out I guess. It's beyond me what all this is about. I just want to get home now to the family, and make sure they are all ok," Henry sighed, and jumped back into the drivers seat of his truck.

The two trucks left, in a mini convoy. The four of them had decided to head into Duntoon together, and see what answers they could find, before heading off to their homes, and their no doubt worried loved ones. Adam and Di rode with Henry, and Jack drove solo, which he was quite happy with.

"I say we go to the main office of the Duntoon Daily Times. If you want to know all the news, then go to the source that reports it," Di suggested to Adam and Henry as they drove down the highway, followed by the old Fella driving the old Bedford.

"Yeah, not a bad idea," Adam replied, "I have a mate who works in the printing department there, he might be able to get some answers for us."

Both trucks pulled up outside the Duntoon Daily Times. The outside of the building was not remarkable, though obviously had much history soaked into its walls. The inside was something quite different, even though the reception desk was only staffed by two administration staff, it was obvious the rest of the building was a hive of activity if all the voices and machinery noise was anything to judge by.

"Look at the people," Jack said to the others as he peered out the window of the large front windows. "Damn fools, shopping, sipping capu-damn-chinos, like nothing in the World is wrong!"

Jack was right. People, in the city area at least, were carrying on their business as normal. Shopping, drinking, eating, laughing, arguing, walking, jogging, loving, sweating in the gyms, and sweating in their lies to one another. A typical day in humankind.

"We are amazing creatures in many respects. The World can be changing around us like never before in history, yet if we can't see it in front of our eyes, it is someone else's problem, and everything will be sweet because we somehow lead a charmed life where nothing can possibly go wrong, until it does," Adam commented to his new friends as they moved further into the Duntoon Daily Times building.

Peter was a typical printer. Had a passion for it, and immersed much of his time in it, almost becoming a part of the giant machine that he was in charge of. He was not a tall man, yet his personality more than made up for his lack of height. Though he could not be described as an intellectual genius, by any means, his likeable personality and friendly nature made him a worthwhile and valued associate to all who knew him. Peter had come out of the printing press room, a huge room more like a warehouse, to meet his life long friend Adam, and the other three where they stood in the general reception area.

"From what I've seen and heard," said Peter to the four visitors "the highways are all closed off, apparently blocked up real good from that storm, and two cops have been killed out near Weston, just near where the highway blockage is."

"Um, blockage? Mate, who told you that?" Adam asked Peter.

"Our Police liaison reporter, who got that straight from the cops themselves. Dude, what else would it be stopping cars getting in and out. You been on the booze Bro? You're not listening to the usual twits spreading rumours about highways disappearing and all that crap are ya?" Peter laughed.

"Never mind," said Adam. "So what about these cops being killed, what have you heard about that dumb ass?"

Adam and Peter were friends enough that insults flowed freely between them, yet never caused offence. This was something that constantly baffled Tricia, and most other women. "Why do guys constantly insult each other, yet are the best of friends at the same time?" the would often ask her friends.

Peter smirked, "I'll Dumb Ass you bro! Well, the official Police information is something about a guy trying to outrun them, and then shot them down when they cornered him where the motorway was blocked. But, how's this for another wacko rumor, apparently a handful of road crew who were there, reckon they found the cops in a field about 200 metres past the highway block, with spears through them!" Adam told the group, with sarcasm in his voice.

"Spears? What the damn heck?" Jack said.

"Yeah, crazy huh?" Peter smirked.

Adam stared at Peter silently, until eventually the smirk on Peter's face disappeared, and he mumbled something about getting back to work "Before I get my ass kicked,"  and wandered back into the large printing press room, leaving Adam, Di, Henry and Jack standing in silence, and with more questions now on their minds than from before they entered the building that housed the Duntoon Daily Times.

# CHAPTER SEVEN

It hadn't been an easy day for Tricia.

Firstly, she couldn't reach her Mother by phone. Secondly, their drive to meet up with her Mother at the Holiday Camp in Oldstown had ended with literally the end of the road for any attempt to get there. Thirdly, she didn't know whether she would ever see her Mum, or Adam again.

Three hours had past since Henry, the highway maintenance engineer had dropped her off at her and Adam's fairly modest though well appointed cottage in Duntoon. Henry had told her not to worry, "Everything will be fine, it was probably some elaborate practical joke by students. You know what those fella's are like," he told her, "always coming up with some scheme to get a laugh, and usually each one is more elaborate than the last," he said with what was supposed to be a reassuring smile, but appeared more as a worried frown accompanied by a smile. Tricia had smiled at him and nodded her head, but she knew this was way beyond a students' practical joke. You can't just make a national highway suddenly stop, and in fact disappear and be replaced by mature tress, bush and other flora. Something had happened that was beyond her reasoning abilities, something had to have happened last night, that dark long night with only the lightning illuminating what must have been the truth of what was happening to them all.

The phone rang. Tricia jumped at the suddenness of the burst of high-pitched tones that sung out from the speaker. She ran to it, grabbed the handset, and before it even reached her ear she was shouting, with a huge smile on her face, "Adam!"

"Hello? Is that Tricia? It's Donna from Duntoon Hospital. You there?"

A tear rolled down Tricia's face as she stood there silent for the moment. "Hello? Is anyone there?" Donna asked again. Donna was a pleasant and very large lady who greatly enjoyed her nursing career. She had become a good friend of Tricia's over the last three years of nursing together, though not so close as to be calling in for drinks or going to parties. But close enough that she could tell by looking at Tricia's face, or hearing the tone of her voice in this case, to know when something was wrong, and to care.

"Yeah, I'm here. It's Trish," the finally managed to get out.

"Oh. Are you ok Trish?"

"No, not really. But, yeah, it'll be ok."

"What's wrong hon?" Donna asked, with an obvious tone of concern in her voice. "Are you sick? Is Adam ok?"

"It's a long story. But you have probably already heard on the news, you know, the highway?"

"Oh, yeah. The blockages? That's why I am calling you hon. I heard the highways were all blocked up real bad from that storm last night, and so I wondered whether you would have got through to the campground. I am guessing it mucked up your plans huh? That's what's upsetting you? I'm so sorry Trish, and now me bothering you."

"Blockages? Donna the whole highway has disappeared! No blockage, just no highway!" Tricia sobbed as she spoke. Not so much for the mystery that had altered her life in such a way she no longer knew what was up and what was down, because the laws of physics seemed to have changed over night, but more so because she was unsure where Adam now was, or whether he was ok.

"Disappeared? You mean under a landslide? Wow, I am sorry Trish, but they will get it cleared eventually."


"No you don't understand, you had to see what I saw to understand." Trish gave up trying to explain. She also wondered, maybe, just maybe it was a landslide, somehow. She couldn't advance the notion any further than 'somehow', and she was happy to leave it at that, hoping this would bring back her World that seemed to have absconded with it's friend, reality.


"Well, you obviously aren't in a state to work today are you? It's ok. It's just that, well, I was asked to give everyone a call who was off today, and see if they could come in. It's like really busy Honey, we have around 20 people who all crashed off the highways, south, west and a cop from the Northern, he's smashed up bad. With him and the other cop, it's chaos here," Donna explained, apologetically.


"Other cop?" Trish asked. Something about those words "Other cop" sent a chill down her spine, though she couldn't quite understand why.


"Yeah, poor guy. He was with the two cops murdered. Did you hear about them Anyway, along with his stab wounds, he is in a real bad way psychologically, we have had to sedate him. He was raving on about people in brown and green gowns or something, throwing spears, and, oh you know, just crazy stuff really. Unless of course, it was crazies who attacked them! You never know these days."


"Ok, I'll work. Give me an hour ok? I need to wash and change, and write a note for Adam." Trish hung up the phone without even waiting for a reply. Maybe Adam's thirst and passion for mysteries had rubbed off on her, as she wanted to see this 'crazy cop' and listen to what he had to say. Or maybe it was more the opportunity for distraction that seemed so appealing and so necessary at that moment.

# CHAPTER EIGHT

Henry dropped Adam home, and as he did so he saw Tricia walking out to her car parked in the driveway.

"There's that gorgeous Mrs of yours Adam. Take good care of her mate, she will be shaken up with all this nonsense going on," Henry said, as both he and Adam looked out the passenger window at Tricia.

"I will Henry, that's a promise. What about you? Where are you going now, and what's next?" "Me? Huh, don't worry about me mate. I'll go check on the family, make sure my Mrs is ok, and fill her in on the crazy stuff we have seen and heard, see what she thinks of it all. Maybe catch up with you tomorrow, if you have nothing better to do than hang out with road crew?" he chuckled.

"Yeah, that would be great man. I need to get some sleep though, real bad. Haven't slept for nearly two days, was going to sleep when we reached the campground, but, yeah, that plan sort of flew out the window."

"Well my friend, I'll call round here tomorrow say 11am, give you time for your beauty sleep?" Henry laughed.

Adam jumped out the truck, and waved Henry goodbye. Tricia had seen the truck just as Henry was pulling out, and driving off. She was more concerned about Adam however, and quickly ran to him, wrapping her arms around him, and telling him how much she missed him, and loved him.

Adam assured Tricia he was fine, and everything was ok now he was home, but she continued to hug him, and he didn't protest. Tricia believed a hug has almost magical qualities when coming from one we love. It emits a feeling of warmth, of togetherness, a feeling that stays with you sometimes for the rest of your life. When we look back, it is often that warmness and delight that is obtained from the embrace of a loved one that fills our memories and our heart. Maybe we won't recall the hug itself, but the effect it had on us seems to affect a part of our soul, and stays there waiting to revitalize our level of happiness and our need to feel wanted, when we so desperately need to feel that way in times of sorrow and loneliness. This hug, was certainly doing more than it's fair share of filling Adam's soul with that very special energy that he was going to need in the coming days.

"Where are you off to Trish? I've missed you so much."

"They need me at the hospital Adam, it's hectic down there, Donna called and said they really need some help."

"Baby, you are supposed to be having a break, and with what's going on at the moment, I would rather you were at my side," Adam told her, frowning in obvious concern.

"What else have you heard, or seen? Tricia asked, sounding nervous about hearing the answer that he may give her.

"Oh, nothing more really from what you saw earlier with me," he said, not telling the full story, purposely so as not to worry her. Yet little did he know that she also held a secret in regards to an injured Police Officer that may have helped to sort out the jumbled jigsaw of a picture that he had in his mind of what was going on.

"I need to go and help out Adam, they really need me there."

"Ok, but I'm dropping you off at the hospital, I want to make sure you get there ok, and I want to see what is going on down there too."

Tricia reluctantly agreed, and they both climbed in Tricia's little car, a 2009 light blue Hyundai Getz. The way of the future in automobile transport appeared to be little cars like this one, much to Adam's amusement. Just before they reached the hospital, three army land rovers, and three army trucks drove past them, heading towards the Western highway. In the back of each were at least a dozen soldiers, all heavily armed. Just as Adam was about to comment about this odd sight, another two trucks drove past, both carrying two NZLAV's, which were the New Zealand Army's armoured and armed troop transport vehicles. Each NZLAV was armed with a 25mm cannon, two machine guns and eight grenade launchers, making them a formidable opponent in a ground based firefight. They were preceded and followed by two Police cars, lights flashing, and clearing the way for a hasty trip to wherever their destination may be. Duntoon had an army battalion based there, along with a Navy reserve, and it appeared that the military in Duntoon was being mobilised, but for what reason, neither Adam nor Trish knew.

"Ok," said Andy, as they pulled into the Hospital staff parking lot, "that tops off the weird and worrying things we have seen today."

"It's really frightening Adam, it really is," Tricia replied, reaching her hand out to Adam's hand, and holding it tightly as he parked the car.

# CHAPTER NINE

Jack had decided during his drive back to the house that he shared with his sister Susan that by tomorrow morning all would have been sorted out and everything would be back to normality. "Had to be those damn students!" he said to himself as he traveled in his old white Bedford truck along the highway. He was tempted to drive to where the highway had seemingly come to an end, and find where the real highway was; after all it was just a "Dumb practical joke" in Jack's mind. Yet he also thought about Adam, Di, and Henry, and worried about them. He even said a little prayer as he drove. "Lord, it's me, you know, Jack, that old Kiwi bloke who fails to follow your rules. But I try Lord, I try, but damn it - oops, I mean, goodness it's hard sometimes. Anyway Lord, I'm not sure what is going on in this strange town, but no doubt it's not that big a deal that you won't sort it out in no time. Well Lord, please look after Adam, and reunite him with his wife. He seems like an all right sort of bloke. Also Lord, that beautiful little lady, you know the pretty blonde one, (he whispered, feeling like a naughty school boy sharing a secret crush with a friend) make sure she gets home ok, and looks after herself, with your help. Also that old codger Henry," he laughed, "Look after his old bones, and have his family give him a huge hug, everyone of them, he's alright Lord. Amen." Jack smiled as he thought about his new-found friends.

Jack was soon pulling into the long driveway that led up to the house. As he did, he noticed two of his goats, Lucky and Bob, were loose and grazing at the side of the driveway.

"Oh damn it Susan," Jack said to himself, "You have left that gate open haven't you."

Jack scrambled out of his truck, and within a few minutes, despite their stubbornness, he had managed to herd Bob and Lucky back into their paddock. It was only then he realised there was something missing. Susan's two horses were nowhere to be seen. Because their small farmlet was based mainly on flat ground, with the only hilly parts being on the outer boundaries, you could see pretty much all the land from most viewpoints around the house. It was also then, after looking harder, he saw Susan, laying flat on her back about 50 metres or so away in the main paddock, not moving.

"Susan!" Jack cried out, as he ran to where she lay, stumbling halfway there, falling to the ground, staggering back up onto his feet. He reached her, and fell to his knees again, this time from the shock of what he saw.

"Oh Susan, Susan, my sweet Sister." Tears formed in Jacks eyes, and began to slide down his face dripping onto Susan, as he held her bloodied body in his arms.

Jack's first thoughts were that she must have been kicked by one of the horses, and was now unconscious, but within seconds of seeing the amount of blood and obvious large entry wounds, he realised this was no accident. Susan had been stabbed at least four times. Susan was dead. Jack's heart sunk, he was struck with grief so deeply that he could barely breath. He had spent almost all his life in close contact with his sister, sharing this property with her for the last few years, this property where he now kneeled and felt his World had ended, and where she now lay where her World and her life had indeed ended, suddenly and violently.

Losing a loved family member affects us all differently, but affects our state of mind and triggers reflections of our relationship with that person much the same. We immediately think of the time we didn't spend with them, the things we didn't say that we should have, and what we did say that we shouldn't have. We yearn to have them back, just one more year, one more month, one more day, even just one more hour, to tell them we love them, we care about them, and we so loved sharing our life with them.

Jack asked himself what so many of us have also asked. "Why? Why now, why my loved one, why like this, and why not me instead?"

Jack sobbed, and hugged Susan's body. He couldn't bare to let her go, despite her blood now soaking his own clothes, and despite the anger and disbelief he had that someone would, could do this to his lovely sister.

"She never harmed anyone, never a bad word to anyone, you bastards, rot in hell you damn bastards!" Jack shouted out, breaking down into an even deeper state of grief as the last words left his lips.

He wasn't a very strong man; despite the years he had worked the land. Yet strength filled Jack in his determination to carry Susan back to the house, he wouldn't allow any more dishonors upon her body by leaving her lying in a field. He carried Susan, cradled in his arms, back to the house and laid her on the couch in the living room. He walked to the phone, thumping his chest as anger now began to consume him.

Jack dialed 111, not sure whether it would go through or not. It did.

"Duntoon emergency. Police, Fire, or Ambulance?"

"Argh," A loud long sob escaped him as he tried to speak. "Oh God. I don't know." Jack cried.

"Sir, what is the emergency, take a slow deep breath sir, and tell me what is wrong," the operator replied back to Jack.

"Oh no, my Susan, someone has killed my lovely sister Susan, why oh why ..." his voice curtailed off, again breaking into only sobs.

"Sir, what is your address, I will request Police and Ambulance attend immediately."

Though the phone systems were working within Duntoon city limits, the computer system that Emergency services used to locate addresses from phone numbers, had lost it's connection with the main server located in Wellington.

"Sir?"

"Sir, are you there?"

Silence greeted the operator. Jack was frozen, phone in his hand, he stared into the kitchen area. Someone was in there, maybe more than one, he had heard creaks, he recognized them as the loose floorboards at the end of the kitchen not quite visible from the living room.

He guessed, in fact he knew, whomever it was either knew who had killed Susan, or was in fact the killer him, or herself. Jack dropped the phone, with the operator still asking for his address.

Jack grabbed the only thing he could possibly use as a weapon for attack, or in defense of his own life, a large book on goat farming that was sitting in the bookcase near where he stood. He was not going to wait any longer, anger took control, and he rushed into the kitchen to catch whoever the "Son-of-a-bitch" was, off their guard.

He rounded the corner, into the kitchen, shouting obscenities.

"Who the hell are you!"

Jack never received an answer, at least not a verbal one. As he took his first step into the kitchen a spear flew through the air at an incredible speed, pinning the book he was holding to his chest, penetrating it by several inches and knocking him backwards onto the floor.

As Jack struggled for breath, two men peered down at him, one with long black unkempt hair, and the other with sandy coloured, yet dirty, long blond hair.

"You damn little girls!" Jack tried to shout at them, but it only came out as a wheezy almost inaudible whisper. "Why the hell you wearing dresses, you damn weirdoes, you killed my sister, didn't you?"

As Jack struggled to get another insult out, the dark haired man in a robe, rather than a dress, suddenly and violently twisted the spear protruding from Jacks chest, and then ripped it out, ripping the last of Jack's life force from him as he did so.

The blonde man said the only two words from either of the be-robed mystery murderous couple that they spoke towards Jack, "Elite scum!" and spat on Jack as one final indignity on this once proud hard working man, who it is fair to say loved his Sister more than life.

With his Sister gone, maybe the two murderers did Jack a favour by ending his now seemingly meaningless life, yet they killed him with hate, not with any mercy intended.

# CHAPTER TEN

Larry and Richie were not in a fit state to be worrying about getting their assignments in on time. In fact, they were hardly in a fit state to walk and talk let alone get themselves down to Duntoon University and hand over Assignment Two 'Robotics in Theory, A Practical Application'.

They were both aged 23, and had been studying robotics and engineering, along with several Information Technology papers for the last four years at Duntoon Uni, and were in their second year of Post Graduate study, working towards a Masters in Advanced Robotics.

"Oh Dude, that JD's is lethal. My head feels like it has a steam engine in it, travelling around and around the inside of my head," Larry complained, though not really expecting any sympathy from his friend and flatmate Richie.

"Don't talk, no noise, hurts my head." Short, punctuated sentences were the best Richie could do for now. "Frigging beer, and JD's, not good."

Within a few minutes both of them had fallen back to sleep, on the couches in the lounge, feeling the World was to blame for their hangovers, after all it wasn't them that invented alcohol.

Three hours passed before Richie woke, saying one word "Coke!" as he reached for a half empty bottle of coke sitting on the coffee table next to him. Sculling almost the entire remaining contents of the bottle, he saved just enough to flick out the end and onto Larry.

"What the hell!" Larry shouted, sitting up as fast as one can when one's head still feels like it is about to explode. "Man, something landed on my face dude!"

"Ha-ha, dumb ass, wake up man, we need to get those assignments in before the 4pm cut off."

"Oh dude, let me sleep."

"Nah, get up before I get a bucket of water," Richie replied, laughing.

Around 30 minutes later, among many more obscenities aimed towards each other, they finally left the flat, leaving behind them what can only be described as a bomb site after it has been vandalised by a gang of thirty juvenile delinquents high from sniffing two litres of glue.

"Tidy up latters?"

"Yep."

After a brisk, and slightly reviving walk to Uni, they entered the Admin building, and deposited their assignments into the post box marked "Robotics. Post Grad. Assignments ONLY." They then walked another 100 metres to the robotics department, and unlocked their lab.

"Larry, mate, where the hell is she?" Richie asked his fellow drinking and study partner.

"What?" Larry replied, always a master of conversation.

"Mate! Otago-Crystal-Mama-001, she isn't on the bench Larry, I'm sure we left her on the bench man. We were going to try to jump start her again this morning - um, afternoon, look the leads are laying across the bench but she isn't! Far!"

"Oh, um, yeah," replied Larry, more preoccupied with why the inside of his mouth felt like a shag pile carpet, and simultaneously gave him a thirst that could only make him think of someone stranded in the Sahara desert for a week with nothing to drink. "I'm freaking thirsty man!"

"Forget being thirsty boof-head, where is OCM 001!"

Otago-Crystal-Mama 001, or OCM 001 for short, was the name that Larry and Richie had given to their Post Grad project robot. Unlike most people's idea of what a robot looks like, or what a robot does, OCM 001 was a square black steel box around 40 centimetres high, and 45cm wide, and did nothing much at all. Out of the top of OCM 001, near a corner was a 20cm high aerial, the rest of the top of robot being mostly taken up by four cavities around 8cm square, each covered with a thick Perspex shatter proof and locked lid. The only other extrusions from its cube like body, excluding underneath it, were two 4cm thick, 10cm long rods, one on each side of it, near the top. Underneath Mama were two rotatable tracks, much like a tractor, that could transport her in any direction and up or down inclines up to about 45 degrees. OCM 001, couldn't actually do anything else but move, but she wasn't supposed to. The project was instead to design a mechanical remote control device that was mobile, and was powered by a non-conventional means, solar power not being allowed. Which is where the four cavities came in, as did part of the name "Otago-Crystal."

OCM 001 was to be powered by crystal like rocks found in some of Central Otago's rivers. Central Otago was a region near the bottom of the South Island of New Zealand, and was a beautiful area populated with many rivers, mountains, lakes, and stunning bush land and forests. These 'crystals', as the budding robot designers called them, were placed into all four cavities, then, or so their theory said, a large electric shock, or 'Jump Start' would be applied to the two rods, which were made of lead. This sudden and massive electric surge was supposed to be absorbed by the crystals, and then the power slowly released over the next 10 to 12 hours through the contacts at the bottom of each cavity, until the crystals were drained of their charge. Unfortunately to date, the theory had proved one big failure. Despite the students applying at least ten shocks to OCM 001 the previous day, the crystals did not hold the charge they theorised they would, and their adopted steel Mama remained inanimate.

"Dude, is that a piece of Mama over there, um, mate, in the wall?" Larry asked a red faced and annoyed Richie.

"Shite! Man, Mama, must have exploded Larry! She's spread all over the floor, and yeah, ha-ha, in the wall! Oh man, did you leave the leads attached to her last night?"

"Oh yeah dude. I turned the power way down to a slow trickle, thought that might charge up the crystals since one massive shock wouldn't."

"Idiot! You blew Mama up Dude! Mate, we have so much work ahead of us to rebuild her, and I guess redesign her".

"Hey man, play back the security film of the lab, lets see when she exploded. I can't see how a slow gradual charge could have blown her up like that, unless the crystals were absorbing power all along?" Larry pronounced, like an excited mad scientist.

Just a few minutes later, the boys had the computer plugged in, and were downloading the security footage from the lab camera, which luckily ran from its own generator's power, like all the other University security cameras throughout the main campus, in case of a power cut.

What Larry and Richie surmised from the footage was the electrical storm the night before had sent a bolt of lightning through a nearby main generator, or so it seemed, sending a surge through the robotics department and into poor old OCM 001, blowing her to smithereens in a fraction of a second.

"Wow!" They exclaimed simultaneously as they watched Mama fly through the air in about a 100 pieces! They then, almost still in unison, said "Oh, uh, what the heck?"

The footage showed OCM 001 being blown apart all right, but then also showed what could only be described as a purple strobe type light come from all four of the crystals' that had been ejected when the robot blew. The purple strobe only lasted a matter of 1 to 2 seconds, but it was like nothing the two Mama-Lovers had ever seen before.

# CHAPTER ELEVEN

Adam accompanied Tricia into the hospital. Seeing the military and police speed past them had unsettled him, and had left Tricia trembling.

"It's ok hon, I'm sure it's probably nothing." He didn't sound very convincing at all.

"Yes Adam, dozens of soldiers, tanks, Police are murdered, the highway somehow vanishes, but it's all probably nothing huh?" Tricia replied, not so much sarcasm as it was a statement of the facts, and that she knew Adam was trying to convince himself as much as her that everything was ok.

Tricia went to the emergency dept., and was immediately placed in triage, which is what she did on most shifts, being experienced enough to know when to rush someone in, or place them at the back of the queue. She also had the type of personality that helped reassure people when they thought they were dying, but in fact had eaten way too much chili-con-carne, without belittling them and making them feel like a fool. She also felt for those who came to the ED with relatively minor complaints, such as flu symptoms, because they simply had no money to be able to visit a GP. The Government of the day had little time for people with little money, and the occurrences of people seeking hospital treatment, which was free for NZ citizens, were increasing by the month as their costs of living also increased yet their wages did not. What seemed partly to blame were the increases in taxes, and subsequently on almost all the prices of consumables, in an apparent bid to 'save the planet' from climate change. It seemed that saving the planet at the expense of many of the planets inhabitants was the politically correct thing to do.

Adam took a seat in a back corner of the waiting room, deciding he would rather try and sleep here, where he could be near Trish, than alone at home with only his racing mind, and their two pet turtles as company.

"In the face of adversity, and in the face of calamity, the only place one should be is near the one they love the most," he told Trish.

"Someone get security!" Adam heard someone shout. Seconds later a man in hospital pajamas ran down the emergency room corridor into the waiting room, screaming and shouting.

"They were everywhere, everywhere! Wearing robes, like some cult or something, they killed Multon and Jones, they just killed them right there where they stood. They had spears, what sick freaks have spears!" He ran back into the Emergency room, arms shaking, sweat dripping down his face, pursued by two nurses, an orderly and a security guard. Adam knew the guard, it was Thomas, and he worked for the same security company as Adam.

Adam approached Tricia who had just finished triaging a patient.

"Who was that?"

"Uh, I think that might be the cop who was with the two who were murdered; I was told he was struggling." Her voice became almost a whisper as she realised Adam now knew she had kept that from him.

"Why didn't you tell me about him, if you knew? You know I'm trying to work out what the heck is going on Trish?"

"Because Adam, it's not your mystery to solve ok? I don't want you getting all tied up with this and ending up like those cops! I need to see the next patient, so go home and sleep ok? Please?" Tricia was virtually pleading with Adam, as she could see how tired and how stressed he was.

"Ok Trish, but I just want to say hello to Thomas first, then I'll get home and get some sleep before I need to come back and save you from this place."

"Hm, ok, look I need to get back to work; this waiting room is not getting any emptier."

Not really believing Adam, but realising she was in no place to argue with him, she gave him a kiss on the cheek and welcomed her next patient.

Adam strode into the Emergency Dept., most of the staff knowing him and saying  "hi", "hello", "good to see you", "you here again", or just giving a knowing and sometimes worried glance.

"Thomas, good to see you man! You on all night?" "Yeah, I was down for patrol at the Uni, but they called me over here to help keep an eye on this poor guy. Man, he's had a tough day alright. They have sedated him off and on, but he's still wired!"

Thomas was a 30-year-old burly 6 foot Samoan gentleman, yet almost always had a welcoming and warm smile despite all the stress that may be around him.

"You think I could talk to him Thomas, you know how I love a mystery, and I think this is a part of the bigger one I have already got myself into today?"

"Ha-had" Thomas laughed, "I knew you'd ask that. Don't see why not now the nurses have gone and he's settled a bit."

Adam and Thomas entered the cubicle where the previously hysterical police officer lay. He was staring at the ceiling, a tear rolling down his cheek.

Adam had always believed that a good measure for how empathic a person is, is to see how they respond to another person's genuine sadness. It is a function of most human beings to immediately give a part, if only a small part of themselves to comfort a person they see is in grief. We feel their pain, and we want it to stop for them. Those among us who are maybe less human, feel nothing, and fail to see why that is a problem. In fact they believe it means they are tougher than others, that's all. Where in reality, they were born missing something, something that makes us who and what we are collectively. They are outside of who the majority of us are, and probably always will be.

When Adam and Thomas saw the obvious pain in the Police Officer's face, pain from the loss of his colleagues, and the failure of those around him to believe his testimony, a small part of both men immediately strengthened his soul. He turned his head, looked at them, and spoke.

"You two, get me out of here, come with me to the field."

# CHAPTER TWELVE

Adam and Thomas agreed to accompany the Cop, who went by the name of Samuel, to the "field" as he called it, but not until he and Adam had some sleep. Samuel, "Call me Sam" had explained to them that the field was where he and the other two officers were when they were attacked.

"We were checking out the weirdest thing. The Western highway had just come to an end, like it just didn't exist anymore from a certain point. I don't know how, but somehow it had been diverted into a field, with trees, bush and even a stream I didn't know existed! We thought we heard some movement in some bush, so we walked through this field towards it, then out runs about 10, 12, maybe more of these men, and a couple of women, all wearing these sort of robes - weirdest freaking thing. They had these spear things, like spears - but, well, they were made of some lightweight metal. We shouted at them to put them down, next minute they were flying through the air. I got hit in the shoulder and thigh, when I fell I must have been knocked out. When I came around, some Highway maintenance guys were hauling me out of there, I could see Multon and Jones," he shook his head, and his voice broke. "They had been hit straight on man, two spears in Jones, three in Multon. Damn freaks, who the hell are they?"

Adam and Thomas shook their heads. They weren't sure what to make of Sam's story, but they believed him, he wasn't delusional, he was just shocked and heartbroken from what he had seen, as they were after hearing his story.

"I'm so sorry." Thomas walked over to Sam, and placed his hand on his uninjured shoulder. "We'll come with you tomorrow, see if we can find those jerks." "We need weapons," Adam added, "If they have weapons, then we need something too, or we are going to get ourselves killed. I have a hunting rifle at home, you have anything Thomas?"

"No way Adam, I don't like guns man. But you take what you think you will need.

Me, I'll bring my muscles," Thomas laughed.

Adam departed the hospital, after checking twice on Tricia. Once home, he showered and practically fell into bed. Surprisingly, he slept fairly well, though his dreams were full of roads ending in forests, people with spears chasing him and Trish, and Thomas standing on an empty Army truck, shaking his head. He thought he was still dreaming when he heard Tricia's voice.

"Adam, honey, thanks for coming to get me," Tricia said softly, smiling as Adam opened his eyes.

"What.... how... did you get home?"

"It's ok baby, Donna gave me a lift. It's 9am babe. Thomas is here, and he said you and him are going to the shops for something?"

"Shops? Oh, yeah, um, yeah need some new stuff for work; you know torches and other equipment." Adam stumbled through his words, still half asleep.

"If you say so."

Within an hour, Adam was ready to go. As he and Thomas had a much needed coffee in the dining room and discussed how they were going to get the rifle to Thomas's 4WD without Tricia seeing, Henry arrived outside. They went outside to greet him.

"Hey fellas," Henry said cheerfully, after Adam introduced Thomas to him, and Henry to Thomas.

"I see most people have cottoned on to the highways being, well, ha-ha, gone!" Henry said.

"What do you mean Henry?" Adam asked.

"Well, people are panicking my friend. They are queued a hundred or so deep at the Supermarkets and petrol stations, I think they have cottoned on to the fact no supplies can get in or out. Planes leaving Duntoon, well, you ready to hear something like you never thought you would?"

"I think after Yesterday it can't get any weirder," Adam replied, with Thomas nodding his head and laughing in agreement. "I've heard the planes that left Duntoon yesterday and last night, well, most returned to Duntoon, but a couple never did. They say, boy how do I explain this, they say, there is nothing out there any more but trees, bush, forests, no buildings, no roads, no people, except what we have here in Duntoon. Now all planes are grounded." Henry looked down at the ground, as though he had delivered news of a family member's bereavement.

Adam looked at Thomas as he spoke. "We need to find those freaks in the robes, they must have an answer for this, because God knows, I don't."

Adam told Henry about Sam, and explained that Thomas and he were going down to the hospital to get Sam, and then head down the Western highway to where Sam said his two colleagues were murdered.

"Well, count me in boys," Henry said. "Nothing else for me to do. The council has told all of us we are on forced annual leave until further notice, they need to sort out what the City Manager and Mayor want to do with us. Looks like they are in charge of everything. Now THAT you should be worried about!" He laughed.

Duntoon's Mayor, Mr Pete Green was a man who could only be described as a 'nice guy', but competent of managing a crisis like never seen before he was not. The City Manager, one Mrs Alexandria Hastings, was quite the opposite, not a nice person, but perfect for managing a crisis as long as it was done her way of course, with little thought about the implications on those to which her plans may effect in a negative way.

The three men headed to the hospital, deciding to take both Tricia's car and Henry's truck, believing that two vehicles may improve their safety later on. Adam firstly tucked Tricia into bed, and locked the house up securely. He assured her everything was ok, and Henry was simply accompanying Thomas and him into town to get the 'supplies', and he would be home around 4pm to wake her up, ready for her next shift she had been asked to do starting at 6pm. On his way out of the house he quietly unlocked his rifle from its secure cabinet, and grabbed some ammunition from a separate locked draw. He believed that if you were to have a firearm in your household, then it should be kept exactly as the law demanded it should be.

On the drive to the hospital to get Sam, Adam saw what Henry had described, queues dozens thick outside of the supermarkets and at the Petrol stations. What Henry had not told him was that at each of these places were at least 2 to 4 armed soldiers, and most also had one or two Police patrols. It seemed they were there more for crowd control, and rationing than anything sinister, though the armed soldiers made Adam feel uneasy. New Zealand was a country that usually had an overall sense of peace, and though it had a fairly high crime rate compared to similar countries, for most citizens their lives were free from violence, and free from seeing armed military or armed police personnel on their streets.

"Guns," Thomas said solemnly, "the epitome of violence. An invention solely designed to bring about death, nothing else. Yet so many claim it is for bringing peace, which is about the same as saying water is for making you thirsty."

"Trouble is Thomas," Adam replied," in these days where the bad guys have guns, or spears come to that, you need to meet their fire power with fire power to prevent death, otherwise they win, and people die."

"People die either way when there are guns, or any other weapons involved Adam. It seems sometimes that people almost want violence to fill a void in their life, and a weapon is the first step they take towards achieving their goal." The conversation had ended with both men looking and feeling depressed and almost defeatist.

Thomas had from a child always believed that it was a strange phenomena that saw those who own guns, and yearn for them, gain such a feeling of strength, power, freedom, and a sense of union with fellow gun owners. Yet the victims and haters of guns only get the feeling of destruction, loss of power, and loneliness from the very same items.

# CHAPTER THIRTEEN

Convincing the head nurse and the Doctors that they would look after Sam, and they simply wanted to "Get him away from all the drama for a few hours" to aid his recovery, was not an easy task. Yet between Henry's "Come on fellas, he'll be right", Adam's "He needs this Doc, you know I wouldn't steer him wrong", and Thomas's smile and warmth, they achieved the desired result.

Sam accompanied Adam in his car, with Thomas riding in Henry's truck. They had one stop before heading on to the highway, and that was for Adam to check that Trish was ok. He silently entered their house, and walked into their bedroom. There he saw Trish fast asleep, and he realised why he loved her so much. She gave him a feeling of calmness, reassurance and fulfilling love just at the very sight of her face. He smiled, and walked back out to the car where Adam waited, ensuring he locked the house door tightly before he left.

"So, the military will now be guarding the field?" Adam asked Sam.

"I guess so. I heard they were seen heading up that way."

"Yeah, me and Trish saw them too."

"Well," Sam said shaking his head," I hope they don't make the same mistake we made, and try and talk with those fools if they come back. They need one type of communication, cold lead." There was a tone of hatred in Sam's voice that gave Adam an uneasy feeling, though he understood that Sam must be traumatized from what he witnessed, and put his comments to nothing but the effects of psychological shock.

"Talk with them? What did you say to them?" Adam questioned.

"Wasn't so much what we said, but what one of them was saying to us."

"They spoke to you?" Adam said surprised.

"Yeah, gave us some spiel, though I can't remember all of it. He was asking us, or more so accusing us, of doing something. He said 'How did you build this so fast? What are you doing here, another Forthold?"

"Forthold?"

"Yeah, and kept referring to us as Elitists, or Elite, or something like that. Next minute, the spears.'" Sam trembled, and turned his face towards the window. He didn't speak again until they neared the end of the Western highway.

-----------------------------------------------

Larry and Richie couldn't help but watch the security camera footage over, and over. What caught their interest the most was the last few seconds just after OCM 001, their so-called robot, had exploded, apparently from a huge electrical surge probably from lightning.

"What is that light man?" Richie asked.

"Beats me Dude, but it comes from the crystals alright. Look at the freeze frame, it comes out of each piece laying on the floor."

They watched frame by frame, the purple light starting as no bigger than a few millimetres in size from the centre of each crystal (which were more rock than crystal), and within two seconds or so becoming so bright it temporarily blocked all view of anything else in the lab as it had overwhelmed the camera sensors. Within about three seconds from the start of the "purple strobe" as the students now called it, it had disappeared completely, with the crystals looking as they always did, completely lifeless and definitely un-purple-like.

"Let's get one of them under the microscope man, see what the heck sent that light out of them," Larry said, suddenly becoming a lot more animated and talkative than when in his hung-over state just thirty minutes earlier.

"Yeah, grab one Larry, I'll get the equipment set up."

Larry, almost breaking into a run, but wanting to look cool, quickly slowed himself and made as best attempt he could as some sort of composure, or at least the best a hungover student can reach as he neared the crystals, which lay on the floor. Reaching down, he went to grab the crystal in his right hand, but when he was still a good twenty or so centimetres away from it, a burst of energy was emitted from the matchbox size rock, jolting his arm and throwing him nearly two metres backwards.

"What the hell!" Larry cursed, "that frigging crystal son-of-a-bitch!"

"Dude!" Richie interrupted, "What happened, you alright?"

"I'm not touching those things man, you get them!"

"Uh, no frigging way Larry. Get the long isolating tongs from the equipment cupboard man, and I'll get a rubber mat. Those things must be carrying one hell of a charge."

Larry fetched the tongs, which were half a metre in length made of lead coated iron, and had handles with 4cm thick high quality isolating rubber. They were used for handling objects that were thought to either be radioactive, or possibly have a foreign substance on them that may be toxic. They were perfect for handling the crystals, or so they hoped.

"You pick it up Rich, I don't want to go near it man."

"Ah, mate, I'm setting up the microscope, you get it."

"Dude YOU get it!"

"Oh for freak sake!"

Richie grabbed the tongs from Larry, strode over to where one of the crystals lay, and reached out to grab it in the tongs.

"Um." He hesitated. "Ma... ma... maybe we should get Professor Co Co Cole in here, and see what she thinks?" Richie said with a suddenly acquired slight stutter.

"Just grab it man!" Larry stated, a lot more confident now that he wasn't the one to have to pick the crystal up.

Richie grabbed the crystal in the tongs, not wanting to look like a coward. He felt nothing travel up the tongs, like he was expecting.

"Huh, Dude, nothing man."

"Um, you have 4cm thick rubber between you and the crystal Rich, you dumbass." Larry quipped.

Carrying the crystal over to the microscope, Richie placed it gently down on the waiting rubber mat on the microscope's base. As soon as the crystal touched the rubber mat, smoke started to pour from the rubber. Thick black smoke began to fill the lab, Richie quickly picked the crystal back up, and placed it down on the concrete lab floor.

"Holy shite!" Richie shouted, "Man, we need Professor Cole dude!"

"I tried to tell you that man"

"Um, yeah right. Go get her before I kick your ass!" Richie shouted, as he backed away from the crystal, shaking his head. "We've either struck gold here man, with these things holding so much charge its like crazy, or this is something so frigging weird, it's going to blow the Professor away."

"It's cool either way," Larry said, as he left the Lab in search of their mentor.

# CHAPTER FOURTEEN

Professor Katherine Cole, the youngest Professor the University had ever employed, didn't really look like a stereotypical Professor, with long light brown hair, bright blue eyes, and standing just less than five foot eight inches, she could be described as no less than very cute. She was also an intellectual powerhouse, having led most of her peers in regards to advances in robotic engineering and electrical engineering. She was also one of the countries top physicists, and few would argue that, simply put, she was one very bright woman.

Professor Cole, or Katie as she preferred to be called, despised Larry and Richie for their typical student hi-jinx, but also respected their drive to look for something different in every piece of research she set them. They truly looked 'outside the box' even though they also delved deeply into beer boxes and got themselves into trouble way too often.

"Pro Cole!" Larry shouted as he burst into the Professors office. "Crystals, man, Mama exploded, freaking shock, oh my arm, Richie said get you!"

"What? Speak in English Larry, with more than one word being greater than two syllables, and form a complete sentence please! This better be good, you don't just burst into my office raving on like a man with a bumble bee stuck in his boxers, and expect me to mark your assignments without prejudice!"

"Ok, sorry Pro. OCM-001, she exploded last night, we think she got some massive power surge, probably from the storm. We tried to pick the bits up, but the crystals Pro, they are carrying some sort of charge, a purple light thingy came out of them, and we saw it on the tape!" Larry burst out with his voice changing tone and volume several times.

"Right, that was almost understandable, but amazingly still made no sense whatsoever. You are telling me something about a power surge, yes?"

"Yeah, yeah. Last night!" Larry replied like a child eager to please his teacher with a correct answer to a problem given to him to solve."

"Will it be easier if I come and see what on earth you and Richie have got yourselves into Larry?"

"Yes, please, Pro. In our lab, you have to see this man, I mean Professor Cole!"

"Katie is fine Larry, as I have told you a dozen times before. Ok, let's have a look at what on earth you are trying to describe."

When Larry and Katie arrived at the lab, Richie had picked up all the parts of OCM-001 except the crystals which all still lay on the floor. He held a Geiger counter in his hand, and smiled at both Larry and Katie as they entered the lab.

"She's a buzzing alright, but just low safe amounts, so don't freak!" He assured them.

"Right, out of here now!" Katie said, or rather ordered.

"Um."

"NOW! Until I decide on whether it is safe to be in here, and work out what the heck has happened. Why do I trust you boys with anything involving electricity?" Katie asked.

# CHAPTER FIFTEEN

Adam and Sam were the first to see the military guards towards the end of the Western highway, around 20kms from Duntoon city centre.

There was a military jeep and a police patrol parked across the highway, blocking vehicular access past that point. Four soldiers armed with fully automatic sub machine guns stood guard, along with two police officers, armed with Glock pistols, and all the men (and the one female soldier) were wearing full body armour.

As their car, and Henry's truck behind them, approached the roadblock, the two Police Officers immediately walked over to them, blocking their way.

"Sorry sir, the highway is closed to all traffic, no exceptions. You will need to travel back to Duntoon, and return to your residence until an official announcement is made," a rather short, though very serious looking officer said to Adam through the driver side window that he had wound down.

Sam leaned across and spoke to the officer. "Andrew, it's me Sam. I want to go and have a look around where we were attacked, you know, sort of get into my head exactly what happened."

"Hi Sam, I'm so sorry about what happened, it's terrible. But look, I can't let you through, strict orders that no one except authorised personnel are allowed past this point."

"Andrew, on whose orders are you acting?" Sam asked.

"The orders come directly from the Mayor, he and the City Council Manager are in charge at the moment, until we get back into contact with the Government and police headquarters."

"Since when can the mayor and city manager order the police and military around?" Adam asked, challenging the officer.

"Since communication with the rest of the country, by telephone, radio, internet, by air, land, water – ceased."

Sam opened the car door, and walked over to Andrew, and the other officer standing nearby. He looked Andrew straight in the eyes, standing less than a metre from him.

"You listen to me Andrew. You are going to let us through. My mates died in that field at the end of the highway, and I want answers! I want to know where those murderous scum went, who they are, what they want, and where they came from. Not you, not anyone, is going to stop me, you hear!"

Sam's raised voice had caught the attention of the soldiers, three of whom now approached him, one with his weapon raised.

"It's ok guys, "Andrew quickly reassured the soldiers "These guys are plain clothes officers, and I know them. They are just coming to do some ob's around the local area, investigating the murders."

Two of the soldiers stopped their approach, though the soldier who had his weapon raised continued towards them.

"I want to see some papers showing me you have permission to travel past this roadblock," the forty something year old soldier barked at them.

Adam, who was heavily involved in a local drama production group in Duntoon, loving any opportunity to use his rather well developed acting skills, climbed out of the car, and walked straight towards the soldier, despite the raised sub machine gun in his hands.

"Who do you think you are soldier!" Adam barked back at him. "Do you know who you are talking to? What is your rank soldier?"

"Corporal," the soldier replied, a little taken back at Adam's directness and seeming lack of concern or respect for his weapon.

"Well, Corporal, I am Lieutenant Detective Adam Wright, and my colleague is Lieutenant Detective Samuel ... Left ... en. ... son." Adam lost his cool a little, and cleared his throat

"Leftenson?" the soldier questioned, with a hint of a smirk on his face.

"Huh hm. Yes, Leftenson is his name, and he is in charge of investigating the murders of the two officers, and I am assisting him. The two men in the truck are  assisting us in our enquiries. Now, move your vehicle so we can get past and get on with our work."

The soldier looked uncertain about what to do, or to think. But when he glanced at Andrew, Andrew nodded his head, not sure what to say about this fairly convincing, though slightly odd stage show.

The soldier lowered his weapon, then turned himself around and strolled back to his colleagues who were now back by their vehicle. After a brief discussion one of the soldiers jumped in the jeep, and drove it to the side of the highway, allowing their vehicles to pass.

Adam and Sam drove through the gap created by the jeep being moved aside, followed closely by Henry and Thomas in the truck.

They had to drive another kilometre before they reached where this highway had ended. An army truck had been parked right at the end of the highway, where the highway now stopped and an overgrown field begun, yet no one was to be seen. Just as they had heard, a house stood testament to the event that had occurred somewhere between 28 and 36 hours beforehand. The house stood just twenty metres or so from the side of the highway, down a cobbled driveway. Everything about the house looked perfect when looking at it from the angle the men stood on at the side of the highway, but when they ventured onto the field that now replaced the rest of the highway for the next hundred metres before it turned into thick bush land, they could see the rest of the house just didn't exist.

The four men strolled over to the house through the long grass of the field. On close inspection they could see the edges of the walls were charred, as were the floorboards, and even half a table, that had now fallen onto its charred edge, as it had lost two legs. The highway's ending edge was also a clean, seemingly burnt cut, just like the Northern highway that Adam and Henry had seen the day before.

"It's as if a giant red hot knife sliced through it at supersonic speed," Adam commented.

"But where are the debris my old mate?" Henry asked  "There's nothing, just this grass and the dirt underneath, not one nail, not one splinter to be seen."

The four men stood in complete silence, except the occasional sigh, and 'tut tut' sound, as they wandered into and back out of the house through the completely open side, standing at times where the house once existed, but no longer did.

Adam had once told Trish "Silence is much underestimated in it's ability to communicate vast amounts of information. Many of us make the mistake of trying to explain something in words, rather than letting silence speak for us."

In this case, the men's lack of words communicated shock and grief, yet acceptance that something incredibly powerful and no less than what must be supernatural had occurred here. If not supernatural, then certainly a feat of such scientific might that it had changed what this part of the World once was, and replaced it with something that was yet to be fully realised.

Sam turned away from the men and looked into the field.

"We need to get the rifle, and plenty of ammunition. If they are still out there, beyond where the bush starts, we are going to need to defend ourselves."

Without a reply, Adam walked to his car and retrieved the rifle and loaded two of his empty canvas pants pockets with ammunition. He joined the three men waiting near the house, and together they walked across the field, heading towards the bush.

"Who do you think they are Sam?" Thomas asked.

"I have no idea. Maybe the same freaks who perpetrated this joke, trick, whatever this is."

"I don't think it's a joke or a trick," Adam said. "This has to be some Government thing, maybe an experiment gone wrong, maybe a military exercise of some sort that has got out of hand. Damn it's cold!"

"I thought it was just these old bones of mine you fellas, but you all feel that chill too?" Henry added.

They all said they had felt the temperature change within seconds of them leaving the highway. Henry buttoned up his fleece lined long sleeved shirt, and rolled down the sleeves. The very warm summer day in Duntoon had ended here, and he wondered whether his sanity had too.

The men soon reached the bush, and started making their way through it. They walked for more than 30 minutes and had seen no sight of anyone else.

"Looks like whoever those murderers were, they have absconded from the area. Shouldn't be surprised really, they weren't going to hang around, " Sam said, with bitterness in his voice.

"No!" Adam suddenly said, in a hushed tone of voice.

"Listen, I can hear people talking!"

They all listened for some time.

"I can't hear a damn thing," Henry whispered.

"Me neither," said Thomas. "How about you Sam, you hear anything?"

"Not sure, thought I did for a moment there. You still hear them Adam?"

"Not now, but off and on, like maybe they are a long way away, their voices might be carrying in the wind, it is blowing towards us."

There was a very strong breeze blowing, and it brought not just a chill in temperature, but also a chill that penetrated much deeper, the chill of the unknown.

# CHAPTER SIXTEEN

Professor Cole had the entire part of the robotic engineering building around Richie and Larry's lab, cordoned off. She had suited up in a full radiation-proof garment, and had entered the lab while Larry and Richie watched via the security camera footage that they now had streaming onto a laptop in Professor Cole's office.

Katie, as she liked to be called, had taken a 'trap' into the lab with her. The trap was a box made from 5cm thick lead, and had a spring-loaded flap at one end, so items could be placed into it, and the lid would firmly and quickly shut as soon as it was released. Katie was also armed with the pair of isolating tongs that Richie had used earlier. The two robotic expert wannabes watched Katie pick up each of the four crystals and place them into the trap that she had taken into the lab on a small trolley, as it was extremely heavy. She then measured the amount of radioactive particles still present in the laboratory air. She took the hood of the radioactive suit off, and gave the thumbs up to the camera indicating it was ok for the boys to enter the lab again.

"So, what now Pro?" Richie asked as he and Larry walked over to the trap, staring at it like it was a cage at the Zoo containing a mysterious rare animal.

"Now boys, we find out what type of charge those things have, and how much of a charge."

-------------------------------------------------

The four new comrades walked towards where Adam believed he had heard the voices coming from. After about five minutes, Adam suddenly hushed the other three again.

"Listen, you must be able to hear them now?"

"Yeah, yeah I can hear them," Sam said.

The other two men agreed they too could hear the voices, which sounded like at least five or six people, men and women.

"Ok, you two stay here, guard this position. We will move out to the East, and sweep the next 250 metres, then sweep back again to make sure we didn't miss anything."

"Will do."

"I think it's the soldiers, what should we do Adam?" Thomas asked.

"We need to approach them, and let them know we are here, we don't want to get shot."

The group walked quickly, though cautiously, towards where they heard the voices. They suddenly entered a clearing, where they saw in fact eight figures, not wearing military uniforms, but long robes, with long sleeves, and some type of thick undergarment covering their legs.

"You, stop or die elite scum!" the tallest male of the group shouted at them.

-----------------------------------------------

Katie ("The Cute Professor" as she was known, though not to her face) had a mind that many thought they had, but was only a figure of their arrogant imagination. She thought quickly, yet acted with great care and diligence, taking into account all possible outcomes of any action she may enact. She believed that too often Women were not taken 100% seriously for their work and ideas, but thought of more-so as a novelty, or something "cute", like, "Oh isn't that cute, she theorised how to run the Earth off of a single re-chargeable battery, now back to our very serious and meaningful discussion about which is the best beer."

Katie didn't let this attitude from the many arrogant and ignorant people who surrounded her at times change anything in the way she worked or how she thought. The Otago crystals that Larry and Richie had somehow turned into batteries holding a massive charge, were just one more challenge and one more puzzle for her to solve, decisively and accurately.

The crystals had been transported back to Katie's own Lab still in the lead trap sitting on the trolley. Larry and Richie lifted the trap onto one of the lab's six benches. Katie carefully lifted the spring loaded flap, and lowered in two electrodes connected to three residual current devices, then her measuring device, which in turn was connected to her laptop.

"This can't be right, my software must have an error," Katie told the boys. "According to this, even with the electrodes not touching the crystals, the power source is reading as over 40,000 megawatts! That's enough power to run a city of about 200,000 people for a few hours! No way."

"Wow, cool as!" Larry said as he stared at the laptop screen.

"Ok, Richie lower the electrodes so they touch one of the crystals."

Richie lowered the electrodes, which were attached to extra heavy-duty wires, down to one of the crystals that lay on the bottom of the trap. As soon as the electrodes touched, there was a simultaneous explosion in each of the three residual current devices, which are designed to absorb sudden electrical surges. The wire connecting all three, and the electrodes themselves suddenly glowed white-hot and the insulating wire turned into ash and black smoke, and then fell to the ground. The wire itself then dripped into small puddles, as it melted. Luckily it appeared the residual current devices and the wire itself had absorbed much of the glancing shock, and left the laptop and measuring device untouched.

"Hit the extraction fans now Larry!" Katie shouted.

Larry hit the switch, and immediately four powerful extraction fans sucked the smoke from the lab within just a few seconds.

"Looks like I need to use my own wire for this," Katie said as she opened a very large steel toolbox that was sitting against a corner in the lab. From the toolbox she took out a reel, with wire that looked to be nearly a centimetre thick.

"This is a copper alloy, copper is one of the most conductive elements known, but I have also blended in some silver, gold and another element which I will keep to myself, which changes it's melting point to around 1600c degrees. Copper usually has a melting point of 1083 degrees Celsius, which with these crystals does not seem to be high enough when exposed to the charge that they are, somehow, carrying."

"Do you think 1600c be a high enough temperature point Pro?" Richie asked

"Well, they don't seem to be doing anything to the lead in the trap, or the lead that coats the isolating tongs, and lead only has a melting point of 327.4c. Yet the last wire we used made entirely from copper still melted. So, I am guessing it is more about conductivity than temperature, but with my new wire, the higher temperature ability negates us trying to work out conductivity issues."

Both the Mama builders looked at Katie with a blank expression. She sighed.

"Ok, what that means in easy to understand language is – this wire wont melt so quickly, yet unlike the lead, will still carry the charge through to our measurement device, hopefully, so we can see what charge the crystals have."

"Oh!" Both Larry and Richie exclaimed in unison, nodding their heads.

"Right then," Katie said, with a little frustration evident in her voice, "get me three of the residual current devices from the toolbox, these ones are also my design, and should be almost indestructible, and will manage any massive charge, or at least to what is measurable."

Ten minutes later they had the equipment rewired, and again Richie lowered the electrodes, also of Katie's design, onto the top crystal.

"Incredible, absolutely incredible! It's recording 400,000 megawatts, and that's just one crystal! But with a charge so high, surely the radioactivity from all four crystals together would kill us almost instantly, in fact we wouldn't have been able to get near them, yet the reading of radioactivity is so low, it's little more than what an average size TV screen puts out." Katie was, maybe for the first time in her life, truly puzzled, in fact bewildered by what she had found.

"You must have done something else with these crystals, damn it - rocks is all they are!" Katie said to the students, with a strong tone of accusation very evident in her voice.

"No Professor Cole, uh, Katie, nothing at all, we just sat them in the slots on OCM 001, then it was that charge, lightning, that's what has done this, we are innocent!" Larry protested.

"He's telling the truth Katie, dude, we sat them on their contacts in Mama, and that was it. When we tried jumping her, nothing!" Richie added. "All that damn corrosion on the silver contacts, that'll be why our charge didn't do it. It took that lightning to get through to the crystals and YEAH they are holding a charge like nothing you ever seen baby! He smiled and gave Larry a high five. Then he saw Katie's face "Um, I mean Professor Cole."

"Corrosion?" Katie asked.

"Yeah, like the silver was so corroded, you couldn't even tell it was silver, that's why we got it so cheap."

"Where did you get it?"

"From the second hand dealers in Cook St. It was an old silver bell, but was seriously black as!" Richie laughed "We melted that Mother down in the lab, and poured it into the slots to make the contacts for the crystals."

"You melted it down, with the corrosion?"

"Yeah, it came out pretty much with a black tint to some of it."

"Silver corrosion, which is really a tarnish rather than corrosion, is also highly conductive. What else did you boys have in 'Mama'?

"Um, well, we did add some promethium into the silver when we melted it," Larry answered, going red in the face and staring at Richie.

"Oh yeah, well, um, only a tiny bit, nothing really!" Richie quickly jumped in to stop Larry from getting them shot on the spot.

"Pro-frigging-methium? That is a radioactive compound, where the heck did you get that!" Katie shouted.

"Well, ha, it's who ya know, not what ya don't know," Richie  replied with a smile.

"Twits! I don't know what you guys have done, yet, and neither do you, which is nothing new. But whatever you have transformed these crystals into, it is like nothing anyone on Earth has ever seen before." Katie gazed at her laptop, her face reflecting off the screen, and her concern reflecting into the atmosphere of the lab.

"Radical!" Larry said, giving Richie another high five, though with little energy, and met with a response from Richie that was more a type of slap therapy than a high five.

# CHAPTER SEVENTEEN

Adam.

Thomas.

Henry.

Sam.

They all froze, with only Henry making any comment.

"Well what do you make of that fellas?"

The eight figures comprised of six men, all carrying spares, and two females, one carrying a spear, and the other with what looked like a crossbow of some sort.

Adam raised his rifle and shouted out at them, hoping his drama skills from earlier in the night wouldn't let him down now.

"No, you stop where you are! We are the scouts for a command unit of 500 soldiers, who are only a short distance behind us. If you want to continue your bad fashion sense for longer than a few more minutes, I would put those weapons of yours down right now!"

Thomas and Sam quickly cottoned onto the bluff, though Henry just looked at him with a puzzled expression.

"Sergent Adam … s," Thomas said, adding the 's' as an after thought when he realised Sergeant Adam really didn't sound quite right.

"Should I call the men now, and surround the enemy, with orders to shoot on sight?"

"No, they aren't stupid; they know the game's up. Put the weapons down, this is your last chancen" Adam shouted again, though his voice breaking slightly as his nerves kicked in.

There was a deafening silence, with the robed eight standing their ground, and the fear-ridden four standing theirs.

Several seconds passed, when suddenly one of the robed men shouted, "Kill them!"

All eight of the spear and crossbow-carrying group raised their weapons, and then appeared to take aim at the four men who had unexpectedly confronted them.

"Get down!" Adam shouted, while aiming his rifle at the same time. He then fired two shots into the male who appeared to be the leader.

He cried out, clutching his chest, and falling backwards hard to the ground. The others, to Adam's surprise, dropped their weapons and all ran to him. They were wailing, and crying out to him "Hastvar, Hastvar! Stay with us Hastvar!"

When they realised he was now dead, most of them began to cry loudly, openly. One of the woman stood, and started walking directly towards Adam, who was still the only one of the four standing, the others laying flat on the ground though their heads raised at the sad yet curious sight in front of them.

Though she held no weapon, Adam didn't know what to expect so her kept his rifle pointed towards her, while keeping an eye on the others at the same time.

She stopped only a metre from him, staring him straight in the face. She was of average height and build, and looked to be in her early forties, not beautiful, but attractivefor her age all the same. Her hair was well kept, and her face and hands looked clean, though obviously not well looked after with moisturisers that most women use. Adam thought he detected some Asian like features to her face and eyes, though only very slight.

"Why!" She said.

"Why have you come here? This has been our land for over 250 years, and now you build another forthold here? Haven't you done enough to hurt us? You even kill

Hastvar, our leader, the one who has taken us through the death-season, and added to our population. Leave us in peace!"

Adam looked at her, bewildered by what she had said. But before he could speak, Sam stood up, and walked up to her and slapped her face, though she barely reacted other than turning her head from the force of the blow.

"You bitch!" Sam shouted in her face. "You were one of the murderers who killed my mates! You crazy woman, you and your friends, damn druggie filth!"

"You Elite, you all deserve to die for what you have done to us, and continue to do!" she replied, seemingly unaffected by Sam's confrontation with her.

Henry walked over to Sam, placed his hand on his shoulder, and prompted him to come back to where Thomas now stood, a few metres away.

"Come on Sam, you need to get some space my friend," Henry said to him.

Sam, after continuing to eyeball the woman for a few seconds, eventually turned and walked with Henry to where Thomas stood, leaving Adam and the woman face to face.

Adam knew he would have to continue the bluff he originally started, and act fast if he was to keep things under control, and keep him and his friends alive. He pointed the weapon away from the woman, and towards her clan who still grieved around their fallen comrade. Adam believed that these people, whoever the heck they were, valued their friend's and family much greater than they did themselves, a noble attribute for sure, but one that would work in his favour, or so he hoped.

"If you don't want another of your friends to die, you go over there and bring me all the weapons you threw on the ground, and do it quickly, or I start killing your friends one by one." Adam gulped, knowing that he couldn't bring himself to kill anyone else, unless they directly threatened his or the other men's lives. Even killing the man, apparently called 'Hastvar' had shocked him. It had shocked him at how easy it was to just pull a trigger, and put a complete and permanent end to another life. To put a sudden end to the person's breathing, thinking, loving was so simple and quick, yet Adam knew would leave an ever-lasting impression on his very soul.

The woman turned and walked away towards where the eight had originally stood, and to his amazement, collected all the weapons, brought them to him, throwing them at his feet. She then walked to her companions, spoke to them for a moment, then turned and faced Adam. The other six, stood up beside her, they then formed a single line, raised their hands above their heads and slowly walked towards Adam, faces tilted down, looking at the ground. Stopping in front of him, they kept their heads bowed, and their hands above their heads as though in surrender.

The same woman spoke to Adam again, "We are your prisoners. Do with us what you will."

Adam looked at his three friends, who all shrugged their shoulders.

"Right then," Adam said, "follow us."

Adam, along with Thomas, followed the group of seven, with Henry and Sam leading the group back to where the Bedford and the Getz were parked.

"Ha, can't see us getting all seven of them in the back of your matchbox car," Henry chuckled. "Can't even see us getting them in the back of the Bedford truck, well not without them all jumping out before we get them to the Police Station."

"I'll check the army truck, see if the keys are in it," Thomas said, walking over to the truck.

"Ha-ha, keys in it? It's the army boy, they hardly ever leave the door unlocked let alone leave the keys in one of their trucks," Henry said to him.

Thomas opened the door of the truck, climbed the two steps to the cab, reached in, and climbed back down with the keys in his hand. Holding them up like a trophy he walked towards Henry, with his big warm smile even wider than usual.

"How things have changed over the years," Henry said solemnly, "Where used to be discipline and standards in the military, now it's all about pushing buttons on computers instead of following rules."

Adam signaled for the mysterious seven to get into the back of the truck, which again they did with little more than a hateful glance at their captors. Adam climbed into the back as well, still holding the rifle.

"Thomas, you ride in the passenger side of the cab, so you can jump out if I need a hand on the way back. Henry, you think you can drive this thing?"

"What, you think an old fella like me can't handle a bigger truck?" Henry replied, with a look of disappointment on his face. "My old mate, I can drive any truck you can think of, without a problem."

"Ok Henry," Adam smiled at himm "Sam, I think it would be best if you take the Getz, drive in front, get us back through the roadblock. Those soldiers aren't going to be too impressed with us pinching their truck, or having seven prisoners in the back of it," Adam said, now sitting on the back of the truck, rifle on his lap.

"You don't think I'm going to leave my Bedford here in the middle of Lala Land do you Adam?" Henry said, looking shocked. "She's my baby Adam, can't leave a baby alone!"

Adam remembered his wagon, his 'baby', that now lay in "Lala Land" number two, after he and Tricia drove off the highway to the North, and were officially introduced to the king of mysteries.

"No, we can't leave the Bedford here Henry. Sam, you ok driving the Bedford, leading the way?"

"Yeah, sure. I'll drive the old bomb."

"Hey, hey nowm" □aid Henry, looking most upset.

"Shut up old man!" Sam replied, almost shouting at him, and then walked over to the Bedford and climbed into the drivers seat.

Adam still wasn't sure what to make of Sam. He realized that he had been through a traumatic event, seeing two of his Police colleagues murdered, and himself being injured, but his attitude towards others seemed more as a product of his personali y rather than of his experience.

They left the edge of the highway, the Bedford leading, and the army truck with a total of one driver, Henry, and eight passengers, including Thomas and Sam in it following close behind. Within a couple of minutes they reached the roadblock, Henry stopped the army truck a good 20 metres behind where Sam had stopped in the Bedford, not wanting to freak out the soldiers and Police before Sam had a chance to speak with them.

Within a few minutes, and after some intense stares at the Army truck by the soldiers and police, Sam jumped back into the Bedford, while signaling to Henry to follow him again, through the roadblock and back towards Duntoon. Henry looked at Thomas, both of them smiled, and Henry put the truck in gear and moved forward.

After driving a few kilometres back down the highway Sam pulled over in the Bedford and stopped, and Henry followed suite.

Sam walked around to the back of the Army truck.

"Adam, what's your plan? These guys need to be charged with murder, so I say we take them to the Duntoon station in Coronation Rd so we can process them, and interview them so we can sort out what's going on in these freaks' minds."

"Sam, I know you want, need, to do that, and it does need to happen. But I think once we get them to the station your superiors are going to take over, and they will send you back to Hospital, where you probably should be right now, and they will take us into custody as well."

Sam thought about what Adam said, and nodded his head.

"So, what do we do with them then? You want to take them somewhere where we can interrogate them ourselves?" Sam replied, with a worrisome amount of menace in his voice.

"Argh, not sure about interrogating them man. But, yeah would be good to see what sense we can get out of them, see what they know about the highway, that house, and well, all this weird crap! Maybe, I know, we take them to the store rooms out the back of Duntoon University, I have the key for the security gates, it's part of my night patrol," Adam told Sam.

"Night patrol?" Sam asked.

"Yeah, I'm a security guard, same company as Thomas works for. The Uni, it's part of my patrols at night so I have most keys for accessing the campus."

"Well, sounds like a plan Adam. Lets go," Sam said. "But, um, I get to interview the bitch by myself." He glared at the woman he had earlier slapped, who now sat near the army truck tailgate, just one prisoner from where Adam sat guard.

Adam, nodded, but was starting to realise that if this was a movie, and there was a bad cop - good cop scene, Sam would definitely be playing the bad cop.

# CHAPTER EIGHTEEN

Like two naughty schoolboys getting a lecture from the principal, Larry and Richie sat in Professor Cole's, Katie's, office near the corner, sullen looks on their faces and fidgeting that only emphasised their nervousness.

"So, promethium huh? Chemical symbol Pm. Atomic number 61. Formed by the spontaneous fission of uranium-238." Katie fired out facts at the boys, like bullets from a gun. No textbooks needed, Katie's mind held more than enough information about almost anything in physics or chemistry. "Highly radioactive. Emits x-rays when it starts to break down. Was your promethium about to start breaking down when you acquired it boys?"

"Ah, um, don't think so Pro. But hey, did we form a new compound or something?" Richie asked, almost seeming to forget his and Larry's "crystals" now sat in a lead box, somehow holding a charge of electricity of around 1.6 million megawatts collectively!

"No, Ag-Pm, being silver promethium, has been formed before, though not sure how you two misfits managed to form this alloy without total disaster. My question is why and how does Ag-Pm, with a dose of silver tarnish, when paired up with some rocks ..."

"Ah, crystals Pro," Larry interrupted.

"Rocks!" Katie glared at him, "Paired with some rocks, somehow then transfer, amplify and store a charge of electricity, seemingly from a lightning strike on a local transformer, into the said rocks, and give those rocks the ability to carry that charge hours afterwards! Not only that, but also only give out a trickle of radiation, and even be stable enough to be picked up by insulating tongs, yet melt rubber and copper wire?" Katie stared out her office window into the University parking lot one story below, hoping that somehow the answer was out there, somewhere.

"Um, well the insulating tongs have a lead coating, and the crystals, um, rocks, don't seem to have had an effect on the lead trap either?" Richie volunteered, hoping to win his way back into Katie's good books, and get off her bad boys board.

"Hm, could be. Lead is a poor conductor of electricity, but then those things seem to be holding a charge of 400,000 megawatts each! So, why doesn't that charge appear to carry to the lead? Anyway, our main questions are: will the charge hold, what can we use it for, and what the heck are we going to do with those ROCKS in the mean time?"

# CHAPTER NINETEEN

The Army truck continued its journey back towards Duntoon, with Henry driving and Thomas riding shotgun, along with Adam who rode in the back playing guard to the seven prisoners. Sam, the Police Officer with vengeance possibly taking dominance over his oath for justice, law and order, led the Army vehicle in Henry's Bedford truck.

Adam found himself not just bemused by how just 36 hours or so before all this he was working his shift as a security guard, swearing to himself about not having his raincoat in the non-forecast storm that hit Duntoon, yet he now sat with seven mystery prisoners in the back of an Army truck! Not only did he now feel like he was in a rerun of a World War Two movie, but he also felt like the screenplay for this movie could have only been written by someone who had been driven insane from watching nothing but Sci Fi movies all day every day since they turned three years of age! To top all of that off, the extras had been given costumes off of a caveman movie that had been influenced by H.G.Wells, writer of 'War of the World's'.

Yet Adam also had other feelings and thoughts as he sat in the truck. He felt both sorry for and angry at the five Men and two Women, who sat there sullen, yet at times with a look of puzzlement as they stared at the truck they were in and at the highway they now traveled down. His sorrow for them came about due to their willingness to surrender their freedom so readily. Certainly they were grieving at the loss of their companion, who Adam had shot dead in self-defense, but it was more than that, it was almost like they had just given up hope.

Adam believed that if there was one thing no Man or Woman should ever give up, it was hope. Often the difference between someone who dies after just 3 or 4 days being trapped in a collapsed building, and someone else trapped who lives on for 6 or 7 days and is rescued alive, is that the later never gave up hope, and the former did. Hope is something that is within us all; it is seated deep within us, and maybe even forms a part of our soul. It waits for us to draw on it, use it, lean on it like a crutch as we wait for the event that is causing us concern to pass. It feeds our need to continue on, no matter what is happening to us externally. Yet so many don't grasp and use hope, they give it up for lost, and at the same time give up their last chance of survival, whether that be survival of life itself, survival of love to be felt again, or survival of a relationship with a loved one that maybe one day, given the power of hope, will be mended. Adam wondered how this group could collectively give up this all-powerful gift so readily and completely.

He noticed that on occasion the Woman who had confronted him back in the bush, and asked the bizarre questions, and who had been slapped by Sam who accused her of the murder of his two colleagues, glanced over at him, if only for a brief second or two. He wondered whether she was frightened for what Sam had said earlier about wanting to interview, or "interrogate" her by himself.

"Hey," Adam said, speaking loudly over the noise of the truck's engine and the sound of the wheels against the highway, and gaining the Woman's attention almost immediately,

"It's ok, I wont let him harm you, honestly. I will make sure you get to the authorities, who will treat you fairly and give you a legal trial. We just want to talk to you guys first, we are really confused and worried about all this highway ending stuff you know, like I am sure you guys must be too." He was being honest, though he was also fishing for any information they may give to him inadvertently, and maybe solve the mystery that had enveloped him and it seemed, all the people of Duntoon.

The Woman looked back down at the floor of the truck, saying nothing.

Adam noticed a couple of the men were sweating, and all but one man had rolled the long sleeves of their robes up.

"Why are you guys wearing such thick clothes in the middle of summer?" Adam asked, though not really expecting a reply after their track record of non-communication since they had been seated in the truck. But one man turned to him, a look of anger on his face. Adam quickly placed his hands on the riffle still sitting on his lap.

"You think you are funny don't you? All smug and sarcastic. I bet you and your little Wife, if you have one, sit in your electronically shielded home in your covered city, nice and warm don't you? While we have to live out there in the cold, all year round. I had to watch my daughter freeze to death last winter, we just couldn't warm her up, it was minus 28 degrees. You make me sick!" the man said to Adam.

"Wow, what the heck are you going on about man? Are you guys in some sort of weird cult thing, where you think you live on another planet or something? Seriously, you guys loose me as soon as you start talking," Adam replied.

The man who had spoken gave Adam a look of disgust, and looked back down at the floor, shaking his head. But now the Woman who had spoken to Adam originally, spoke to him again.

"Enough of your games elite scum, just hurry up and kill us!"

"Kill you? What the hell? Look, I feel terrible about shooting your friend, honestly, I have never killed anyone before in my life, but you guys were going to kill me and my friends, I had to do something!" Adam replied.

"Shoot?" The Woman asked, "Why are you using that weapon, what is it anyway? Why aren't you using your normal weapons, they would have taken us all out in a second without a problem. Is this your new weapon of choice, that inflicts a horrendous open wound to act as a warning to the rest of our people?"

"Nope," Adam said, "Lost me again, no idea of what you are talking about. No idea at all." He shook his head, smiling to himself about how ridiculous the conversation he was attempting to have had just become.

The two trucks pulled up by the security gates that led to the storage buildings of Duntoon University. Adam jumped off the back of the Army truck as Sam, Henry and Thomas walked over to talk to him.

"Thomas, will you hold the rifle and guard these guys while I get the gate unlocked?"

"I'd rather not hold that thing Adam, you know how I feel about guns."

"Here, let me do it," Henry quickly offered.

Adam guessed Henry offered due to his concern about Sam being the only other one who could hold the rifle, not knowing what he might do to the seven in the back of the truck, given half a chance.

Sam stood with Henry as Adam and Thomas walked over to the gates.

"Strangest thing," Adam said in a hushed voice to Thomas, "□s we entered the city area, those lot looked as frightened as a rabbit staring down a shotgun barrel. They were nudging each other too, pointing at the buildings, cars, and pretty much everything we passed."

"Did they say anything?" Thomas asked.

"Well, they were mumbling to one another, but with the noise from the truck and other vehicles passing, I couldn't really make out what they were saying."

"You think they are planning something Adam?"

"I don't think so, it was more like they were puzzled, scared, I ... I'm not sure, it was just very weird."

After Adam unlocked the hefty padlock chaining the two large gates together, he and Thomas pulled the gates wide open to allow entry to both of the trucks.

"Thomas, there is one building that is completely empty other than tables and chairs, it has large meeting rooms, as well as bathrooms and at least a couple of kitchens. I say we take them into there for now, they can use the bathrooms if need be, and we can make sure they get something to eat and drink while we hold them there before we take them to the cop shop,"

"Sounds like a plan Adam. Hey, you don't think we will get in trouble for kidnapping or something do you?"

"No, I'm pretty sure we will be ok. After all, Sam is with us, and these guys are basically in his custody under suspicion of murder. We can argue that we brought them here first, because with all this drama, we thought the Police Station would be too busy to handle them right now," Adam reassured Thomas, who looked decisively worried. Thomas wasn't the sort of man to break the law, not even inadvertently. He came from a strongly Christian family, his Father being a Tongan Pastor.

They soon had the trucks in the fenced-in area, and Adam relocked the gate behind them. They ushered the seven captives into the building Adam had earlier described to Thomas. On entering a large meeting room with four large tables pushed together in the middle of the room, and 14 chairs surrounding the table, again with no protest, other than unfriendly expressions, the seven sat down in the chairs around the table. Henry fetched himself a seat that he placed at the only exit, and sat there still holding the rifle. Henry looked quite proud, he felt like he was needed and wanted, something that when we get to an older age few of us get to experience.

Adam and Thomas sat at the table opposite the seven, but Sam paced back and forth, looking hatefully at the group, and particularly at the woman he had earlier accused of the murder of his fellow officers.

"Who are you people?" the woman suddenly asked, staring at Adam.

"What?" Adam almost choked, "Who are we? We want to know who you are? Why the weird clothes, the weird behaviour? I mean, come on, you were going to throw frigging spears at us!"

The woman appeared to ignore what Adam had said, and went on with her own line of questioning.

"Is this some sort of joke? Or is this yet another hoax, trying to encourage our people into this un-shielded city? The ancient buildings, like this one, the ancient vehicles, everything - I don't know. Whatever this is about, it's not going to fool anyone!"

Adam stared at Thomas, Thomas stared back at him, both of them lost for words, but Sam apparently was not lost for words at all.

"You think you are clever coming up with all this crap? Think you are going to plead insanity to the murders huh? Well it isn't going to work, we have you nailed, you hear me?"

"Look," Adam quickly interrupted Sam in his verbal tirade towards the woman, "It seems that you guys are as puzzled as to who we are, as we are about you. I'm not sure whether you guys are being straight up or not, but I am. I'm Adam, this is Thomas, we live here in Duntoon, both security guards, my Wife is a nurse, Thomas's wife is a chef. Henry over there, is a roading engineer, and Sam, well, as you probably know, he's a Police Officer."

The Woman looked at the man seated next to her, he whispered something in her ear, she whispered something back.

"Duntoon?" she said, "What do you mean you live in Duntoon? That city ceased to exist hundreds of years ago."

Henry, still sitting by the exit, laughed, though he quickly ceased laughing when he realized no one else was.

"Ceased to exist?" Adam asked, trying not to say it sarcastically.

"Something is wrong here," the woman said, "You people are different from the Elite I have come across in the past. You dress very different, you talk different, and you even look a little different. This place - it's not like the Elite cities I have seen, admittedly from a distance, but they look far different from this place. This city was also built so fast, just a week ago we came through this area, but other than the purple haze we saw nothing, yet now a city is here."

Thomas looked at the woman and asked, "What's your name?"

"Edotha." she replied.

"Edotha ..." he hesitated, and looked directly into the woman's eyes, and in all seriousness said, "What planet do you and your people come from?"

Henry laughed again, and even Sam had trouble not smiling with amusement.

The woman waited about 30 seconds, then with just as serious a face and voice replied "Earth, where do you come from, Uranus?"

They all laughed except Sam, and Thomas who just looked embarrassed.

"Yep, that's just a joke that doesn't die," Adam said, laughing as he said it.

"Well, I was serious guys," said Thomas, looking a little offended. "I mean, they say they have never seen anything like our city, like us, so how else do you explain this?"

"I'll tell you!" Sam blurted out, "They think we are going to believe some sob story about them being country yokels or something, just protecting their land, thinking they can kill two cops and get away with it. Well, I've had enough of this, the bitch comes with me now down to the Station, where she is going into a cell, and will wait for her punishment. I mean her trial!"

With that he headed around the table, striding directly to where the woman sat, but before he got anywhere near her the five robed men stood up, and surrounded her and the other woman, like a wall.

"Out of my way!" Sam demanded.

They didn't respond.

Sam rushed at them, trying to shove them out of the way, but two of the men grabbed him and threw him on the floor.

"Hey, hey that's enough!" Adam shouted, as he and Thomas rushed around, expecting a mass escape attempt, or at least expecting them to lay into Sam. But instead they formed their wall of bodies again in front of the two women, protecting them.

Sam got up off the floor, in a rage he walked over to Henry and held his hand out.

"Give me that bloody gun!" He demanded.

"I don't think so son," Henry replied. "The last thing an angry man should ever have is a weapon."

"Give me the god damn gun Henry!" Sam shouted.

Thomas came up behind Sam, and put Sam's arms behind his back.

"You mate, need some time out." With that, he edged past Henry who was now off his chair, and took Sam out the door over to an office, pushed him in there and held the door shut, much to Sam's loud protests.

People sit down, please! Look, we are all human beings, that's one thing I am sure about, its a strange time alright, but hey its not the time of savages fighting, its 2012, when we are supposed to be civilised, so lets act it." Adam said.

The robed ones sat back down, the woman though stood. She paced around for a few minutes, while Adam, and Henry watched, somewhat amused by her actions.

She then walked up to the table again, she looked at both the men who were her captors.

"You said it is 2012? What is going on here, it's not 2012, its 2367."

"Well, I'll be Puha in a pot!" Henry said

"Yeah, Puha," Thomas added, overhearing the conversation from the corridor where he still stood, still holding the office door shut which was across from the open door of the meeting room.

"So, Edotha, not wanting to sound rude or anything, but um, what the hell! Two thousand three hundred and what?" Adam said, almost shouting.

"Sixty-seven. The year, for us, is two thousand three hundred and sixty-seven," Edotha replied.

"Ha-ha, prove it," Henry smirked as he spoke. "No offense love, but we have a little bit of trouble believing in time travel."

"I don't know how I can prove it. However, you are telling me you are not part of the Elite, which we have more than a bit of trouble believing. So, you prove it, you prove you are not the Elite." Edotha looked at her companions who nodded in agreement.

"So, how would we do that?" Adam asked

"Simple, lift your hair on the left side of your head."

Adam had long hair for a security guard, certainly not shoulder length, but it was very thick and what could only be described as straggly. Henry, for an older man in his early sixties also had a thick head of hair. Sam and Thomas, both still preoccupied outside of the room, Thomas in the corridor holding the door handle of the room that Sam was temporarily imprisoned in, both wore beanies on their heads.

"Ah, what do you mean Edotha? Why on earth would me playing with my hair prove I wasn't one of these Elite guys you are talking about?" Adam asked.

"Just do it. Lift your hair, and let me see the left side of your head!" Edotha spoke sternly, appearing to be losing her temper, as if she believed Adam was purposely trying to stall her.

"Ok, whatever pushes ya button lady." With that Adam grabbed clumps of his hair, lifted it, parted it, and brushed his hand through it until his head almost started to sting. "There, you happy now?"

The seven prisoners looked stunned. Edotha stood, and walked around the table to Adam, she ran her fingers over his head again and again.

"Hey, hey, that's enough, flipping heck!" Adam protested, "I don't have nits you know!"

Edotha looked at the man who had earlier whispered to her, and her to him. "He's telling the truth, he isn't an Elite!" She then walked to Henry, though he still held the rifle, she quickly ran her hands over his head. "He is not one either, they must be our people, or it's a trick, or ... they tell the truth, they are not from our time!"

"Ok, so now we have played our part of the game, prove to us you are from 2300 and whatever." Adam said.

"67, 2367, I have already told you twice!" Edotha replied.

"Eo, show them," Edotha said to the male who now sat almost opposite Adam.

"Uh, hang on a minute; I'm not sure I want to see! What's he going to show us little lady?" Henry smiled.

The man named Eo turned so the left side of his head was visible to Adam and Henry. He then lifted his long black hair that hung almost to his shoulders. There, clearly visible was a small bald spot, in the centre of which was a silver coloured circle that had a gentle glow coming from the centre of it, almost like the glow from a light-bulb that has just been switched off. It wasn't like a stud as it was completely flush with Eo's skull, with the skin grown neatly and evenly around it, with no scarring evident.

"What the heck is that?" Henry gasped.

"Oh, my, goodness. Adam, you ever seen anything like that? I'm getting Thomas!" a very flustered Henry said, and handed the rifle to Adam, then rushed out the door and walked over to Thomas, excitedly telling him what he had seen.

"You really don't know?" Eo asked Adam, with disbelief evident in his voice.

"Seriously, I have never seen anything like that before that wasn't part of the inside of a computer or something, I mean, nothing I have seen before looked like that thing!"

Eo looked at Edotha, she in turn sat back down next to him.

"Eo is an outcast from the Elite. This is why we call him Eo, as in E.O., Elite Outcast. All the Elite have inputs; an input is what you see in the side of Eo's skull. When you are in an Elite city, or within 200 metres of one, you can connect with the mainframe that contains all the knowledge and history of humankind until now," Edotha explained to Adam, though she looked almost sad as she spoke, like she anticipated his disbelief and wondered if he thought she and the others were insane, as she thought he may be.

"So, who are these Elite you keep talking about?"

"They ..."

Before Edotha could answer Henry and Thomas burst back through the door.

"Adam, he's gone!" Thomas shouted.

"What? Who?" Adam replied.

"Sam, Sam's gone. When I got Thomas to open the door so I could tell him about what we had seen, he wasn't in there, just an open window," Henry explained.

"Shit! He'll be alerting the cops no doubt. We need to get out of here!" Adam said.

He looked at Edotha, Eo, and the others.

"Can we trust you? Are you being honest with us? Do I need to keep this gun on you lot?"

"We tell the truth. I really don't understand this, just like you also seem to be confused by our meeting, but we will trust you, if you will trust us?" Edotha told him, looking also at Henry and Thomas as she spoke.

"I believe her Adam, she has an honest face," Thomas said, with sincerity in his voice, though his warm smile had faded from the strangeness of the day so far.

"Henry?" Adam asked.

"I don't think we have any choice but to trust this lot Adam. They seem genuine, very strange, but genuine," Henry replied.

"Ok, right, lets find somewhere else in the storage area where we can hide; there are another two buildings like this one, and several warehouses. Follow me." Adam started towards the door, and then stopped momentarily. "I'm going to hang on to the rifle for the protection of all of us, don't let me down people."

They all walked quickly from the room, down the corridor to the main exit, and as they started into a slow jog through the door Adam ran straight into someone just outside the building.

"Holy!" He shouted, as the rifle was knocked out of his hands.

As he picked himself up off of the ground, he saw another figure pick up the gun.

"Wow, dude, a rifle!" someone said with obvious youthful excitement in his voice.

# CHAPTER TWENTY

Tricia checked her watch again, it was nearly 4.30pm and Adam wasn't home like he had promised her he would be to take her to work. She had tried his phone several times, but no answer. She was worried about Adam, the man she had married, the man she loved as much as any woman could love a man.

Trish had once told Adam that being separated from the one your heart is dedicated to can unsettle a person to such a degree it feels like someone has picked up your life and shaken it until it was so disorganised, you can't imagine how you could put it all in order again. Yet when that person is reunited with you, the bits and pieces that were out of place usually start to get back into order once again, piece by piece. But until that person does join you by your side, you really start to wonder when or if they will ever be back again. She explained to Adam that this was how her life felt when he was away from her. Tricia was feeling at this moment just as she had described to Adam, despite it only being 30 minutes past when he said he would be back home.

She walked over to the house phone, which appeared to be working fine for calls within Duntoon, and called her friend Donna who was due back on shift the same time as she was.

"Donna, it's me, Trish. Adam has my car, would I be able to get a lift into the hospital with you?"

"Sweetie, of course you can. Everything ok?"

"Yeah, yeah everything is fine, except, you know, all this crazy stuff."

"Yeah, it certainly is crazy alright. I have heard the Mayor is to make an emergency statement to the whole city live on the local TV station and radio at 7pm tonight. Now THAT, we must hear, hopefully it will give everyone some answers."

"Let's hope so."

Of course everything was not fine in Tricia's World. Her husband wasn't home, like she so needed him to be, her Mum couldn't be reached by cellphone or by any other means, and she wondered whether she had simply vanished as the highway had, and it seemed like the whole World outside of Duntoon might have met the same fate.

As Trish walked to her room to get her nurse's cardigan, the power went off.

-------------------------------------------

Larry picked up the rifle and held it above his head, shouting "Yeah, baby!" with a dopey smile on his face like a schoolboy who just found a ten dollar note on the street.

"Put that down right now!" the professor shouted at him.

"Sorry Katie," Larry said, with a disappointed and disheartened look as he carefully put the rifle back down on the ground where it had landed after Richie had collided with Adam as Adam ran from the building leading the others.

Richie had been pulling the cart that had the 'trap' on it, which in turn contained the four 400,000-megawatt 'rocks', as Katie had called them.

"What, who are you, and what are you people doing with a gun?" Katie demanded an answer, though her eyes gave more the message of confusion rather than question, as they darted from rifle to Adam to the robed seven. "This is a secure University area, and you lot are trespassing no doubt. What are you doing, making a student movie I suppose?"

"Long story. But don't worry, I'm a security guard, this is part of my patrol, these guys are, um, just friends," Adam replied.

As Adam spoke the power went off, but within a few seconds the lights that had been on in the buildings came back on.

"Oh, a power cut, the emergency generators have kicked in," Adam said.

"Forget about the power, and though I don't believe that story of yours for a moment, I think you ..." before Katie could finish her sentence, Eo dived onto the ground, grabbing the rifle. He held it up, gesturing to his robed colleagues to stand behind him.

"Ok, now I give the orders, you hear me! All of you get back into this building, move!"

All of them reluctantly but steadily made their way into the building where all but the two students and the Professor had just exited.

Richie started to walk past Eo, into the building pulling the cart behind him.

"Stop, what's in the box boy?" Eo asked Richie.

"Ha, too hard to explain, um, just some rocks."

"Rocks? Why would it take three of you to move a box of rocks?" Edotha asked him.

"Katie? You want to try and explain this?" Richie pleaded.

"They are highly electrically charged rocks, we were transporting them to a secure storage building, safe from harms way until we decide on how to proceed with them," Katie tried to explain.

Edotha looked at Eo.

"Crystalline Mountain Quartz?" Edotha asked Eo.

Eo walked over to the lead box, the 'trap'.

"Open the box, let me see!" He said to Richie.

"Argh, I'd rather not man, those things are like dangerous as □"

"Do it!" Eo pointed the rifle at Richie.

"Chill out Dude!" Larry interjected. "Here man, I'll open the box if ya want to see the damn rocks."

Larry lifted the spring-loaded lid enough for Eo to see into the box. Eo turned to face Edotha again.

"Yes, CMQ. It has been charged, I can feel the power coming from it through my input," Eo told her, excitement in his voice.

"What a day, we find apparent time travelers, access their city, and now we have the power source the Elite use to run their cities. Eo put the weapon down, these people mean us no harm, and they have no idea of what they have here. I also believe they really are from 350 years in the past."

"What?" Katie said in astonishment, "You think you are from the future?"

"No, I don't think we are from the future, but it looks as though you are from our past. In fact it looks like you and your whole city is from our past." Edotha said, a smile finally settling on her face. "Looks like we have a mystery to solve between us all, as well as an opportunity for a new life my friends."

-------------------------------------------

Donna beeped the horn of her Toyota Prius as she pulled up outside Tricia and Adam's house in Duntoon.

Trish rushed out to meet her in the driveway, it was 5.30pm, and they were due to start their shift at the hospital at 6pm.

"Hi Donna, thanks so much for picking me up, I don't know where Adam has got to, but I am sure he's fine," Trish said to Donna as she climbed into her car.

Donna looked at Trish, her face was pale, and she looked as though she had been crying.

"Donna, are you ok?"

"Chaos. Trish, its chaos out there, you won't believe it."

"What do you mean?" Trish asked, concerned for her friend's well-being.

"The petrol stations are all closed, they have soldiers guarding them, same with the supermarkets, in fact almost all the shops are closed.

Earlier it was the opposite, hundreds were queued at the shops. Police are now patrolling the streets in the city area, armed. They even have soldiers carrying God awful looking weapons down the main street." Donna shook as she recounted what she had seen.

"It's ok Donna, we can get through this, that's what friends are for."

Trish truly believed a friend is someone you know will always be there for you, a shoulder to cry on, a laugh to share, and memories that are collected together and treasured always. A true friend will not stab you in the back as soon as you are out of earshot, but instead will defend you to the death, without ever expecting a thank you because they know you would do the same for them.

When Donna had finished with the catharsis of her emotions that had built up as a result of the traumatic events she had witnessed on the drive to Tricia's home, she started their journey towards the hospital.

Tricia observed much of what Donna had described. They passed a large shopping complex where two major shops were located close together, separated only by a car park, which also surrounded them. The carpark was empty other than an armoured personnel carrier, six soldiers and two Police officers who stood guard at the entries to the shoppers' carpark, thereby barring entry to the shops themselves.

Many houses looked like they were locked up tight, with their inhabitants hiding themselves away from the mystery that encapsulated the city, hoping the 'head in the sand' strategy would work for them, though knowing it was as effective as it is for ostriches but wishing for a different result this time, somehow. For others it appeared that family had all gathered in one location, with some family members sitting around outside or pacing back and forth, with little to say to each other. Yet others could be seen sitting at their outdoor furniture, glasses of wine in hand, chatting about their own self importance, and believing as they always had that their copious amounts of money (much of it loaned or imagined of course) would see them through anything, including this - whatever 'this' was.

"What do you think the mayor is going to say tonight on TV?" Donna asked Trish.

"I'm not sure, maybe telling us what on earth has happened, and what this is all about."

"What does Adam think has happened? He must have heard something through his security contacts?"

"I'm not sure. Come home with me after our shift, and we can talk to him together – if he's home." Trish looked down, picking fluff from her skirt, wondering if she would ever see Adam again.

As they drove down the one-way street that led them in the direction of Duntoon Hospital, they were confronted by a roadblock comprised of a Police car parked across the lanes, and road cones blocking any potential attempt to go around the vehicle. Two Police and two soldiers stood guard.

A rather short and young policewoman spoke to Donna through her driver side window.

"Evening ladies. Sorry but there is now a curfew, and everyone is required to stay in their homes until further advice from the mayor."

"A curfew? But we have to get to work, we are both nurses - as you can see by our uniforms," Donna told her.

"So, you are about to start your shift?"

"Yes, both of us work in the Emergency Department."

"Ok, all essential personnel such as nurses are not subject to the curfew if they are working. I'll move the cones, and you can continue, but straight to the hospital then straight home after your shift finishes."

They drove on, the two soldiers eyeballing them as they drove past, one soldier winked at Tricia, who attempted a smile in response, but her lips wouldn't cooperate and the result was more of a worried grin than a smile of acknowledgment.

# CHAPTER TWENTYONE

Katie stood, pacing around the large room, while Adam, Henry, Thomas, Richie and Larry sat at the table with Edotha, Eo and the others.

There was no talking for a few minutes, other than Katie muttering occasionally, as if analysing what she had been told by Adam and Edotha about the interactions so far.

"2367.... highway disappeared .... spears .... crystalline mountain quartz ... powers cities .... gun!" she said to herself.

Larry and Richie had occasionally stated, "Cool, awesome, excellent, sick as!" As the story had been told to them, but after a stern look from Katie they decided to contain their excitement to the odd high five between them, and an occasional slap on the back.

"You guys, you aren't having me on, are you?" Katie asked the group sitting at the table.

In response, Eo stood, walked over to where Katie stood, took her hand in his, though she was reluctant for the interaction of touch with this man she just met. He then ran her fingers over his head, over where the input was located. Katie flinched as her finger ran over the cold steel that was a part of Eo's skull. She then made a clear space in his hair and stared at the silver input with the small central glow emanating from it.

"Amazing, this isn't from our time, this is technology far in advance of what we have." Katie stared at Adam and said, "They are telling the truth ... I think."

"I believe they are," Thomas said. "I can see honesty in Edotha's eyes, she is a trustworthy person I'm sure." His warm smile had returned, and Edotha responded in like back at him.

"Tell us more Edotha, tell us about these Elite cities you say are powered by the, what did you call those rocks, CMQ?" Katie said to Edotha, as she joined them at the table.

"Yes, CMQ. But they use very small amounts, about a third of the size of one of those that you have will power a city for months once it is charged."

"Charged? How do they charge them?" Katie asked, her eyes wide in anticipation of knowledge she didn't think she would ever be a party to gaining, as she had no idea this technology even existed.

"I am not a hundred percent sure. Eo, you explain it. Eo is an Elite Outcast, he grew up in the city nearest where we are now, he took in much information via his input, but he was exited when he was only 20 after he questioned the leaders. Eo, please, tell them what you know of how the CMQ is charged."

"CMQ began to be mined back in the early 2000's, around 2045. There was a discovery at some University in New Zealand that when charged with a massive yet controlled amount of electricity, while in contact with silver promethium, it absorbs electricity and somehow reproduces it as the power is drawn from it. It can continue to do this for up to around six months before it simply crumbles, and needs to be replaced. The Elite now use a liquid silver promethium alloy that they dip the CMQ into while using current control devices and weather control to elicit a lightning strike. This charges the CMQ safely. They use only small pieces as large pieces charged like this, can cause massive explosions. How did you charge such large pieces safely?" Eo asked, looking concerned.

"Eo, much of that made little sense to me I am afraid, though I am sure as time goes past I will better understand. The charges on these CMQ rocks were made accidentally by my two students here," Katie replied, as both Larry and Richie smiled with apparent pride at their "accident".

"Ok, this is all very interesting," Adam interrupted, "but uh, how on earth did you guys get back here in 2012, when you are from 2367?

"We didn't get back here," Edotha said. "This area has been what we thought was an Elite shielded area for many hundreds of years, until the night before last, when we were hunting, and noticed the purple shield had gone, and in its place the strange black surfaced road, and then we saw the ... we thought ... Elite guards."

Adam was going to speak, but Larry beat him to it.

"Um, did you say purple?" Larry asked.

Eo stood, and answered him.

"Yes, the Elite shield their cities with an electronic type shield that is usually almost clear, just a slight cloudy colour, yet the shield around here, where you are, was a thick purple coloured haze, nothing could penetrate it. The local elders say that men first tried to enter the purple haze, as we called it, 357 years ago, and were turned to ash immediately that they touched it. Since then, it has been a no-go zone for us, and we simply hunt around it".

"357 years ago ... 2012," Adam mumbled.

Larry looked at Richie, he then leaned over to him and whispered something to him, Richie replied with a "Yeah, dude. I wonder man?"

"Tell us what you are saying Larry," Katie directed.

"Well Pro, when we watched the tapes of Mama-001 exploding, a purple light came out of the crystals ... rocks ..., um, CMQ, and these dudes say there was a purple haze around the city until now, so you know, um, I don't know." Larry stuttered and choked as he spoke, like he was overwhelmed by the numerous possibilities that all of this information could mean.

"I need to think," Katie said, "I really need to think about all of this."

-------------------------------------------------

Tricia and Donna had arrived at the hospital, it was now 6.45pm, and the ER was remarkably quiet. The two good friends had chatted after they left the roadblock about how they believed it would be chaos when they arrived on shift, but from the lack of patients and activity they were obviously wrong.

Trish left her triage spot for a while as the waiting room remained empty for the first twenty minutes after she arrived, and she walked down to the staff tea room only ten or so metres away.

"Heya Trish!"

Trish turned to see George, the head orderly for the Emergency Department. George was an unusual looking man. He was in his early fifties, but still wore his hair like a teenage hippie, long and scruffy, though he had it tied up in a ponytail when on duty. He was of European descent, though spoke with a Maori accent as he was brought up by Maori Foster Parents, who loved him like their own. But the most striking feature of George was his thinness. He looked like the sort of person who would simply snap if a feather blew into him in a strong wind, yet he was able to push heavy hospital beds without a problem.

"Oh, hi George. You working extra shifts too?" Trish asked.

"Nope, just my normal. Boy it's quiet tonight, especially with no power in the city, and cops and soldiers everywhere. Lucky this hospital has good generators."

"How long can we run on generators though George?"

"Oh, about 5 days I think. They should have the main power back on within a few hours though hopefully,"

"I hope so, I was thinking we would need the heaters on at home tonight, it's got so cold." Trish said to George, who was busy putting his fifth spoonful of Milo, a hot chocolate drink, into his cup.

"Tell me about it! I heard on the local weather station we have dropped to 8 degrees today, crikey it was like 25 just a couple of days back."

"Yeah, it's strange ..." Tricia's voice tailed off as she remembered the field where the 'big green monster', Adam's station wagon, had landed after it left the suddenly ending highway. "It was so cold there, but on the highway it was still quite warm," she thought aloud.

"What's that Trish?" George asked.

"Oh, never mind, nothing really."

"So, you see the UFOs?" George laughed.

"UFO's? What do you mean?"

"Some of the nurses who just walked in for their 7pm shifts in the ward, said they saw lights whizzing over the city just before they arrived at the hospital, and one of the patient's visitors who arrived a few minutes ago said the same thing. Man, today is getting weirder by the minute." George laughed to himself again, and walked off, no doubt down to the orderly's office where they often sit together, gossiping about whatever orderlies gossip about.

"UFOs?" Trish muttered, again talking to herself, which she was beginning to worry about, "What next!"

# CHAPTER TWENTYTWO

Adam had advised the ever increasing group it was time to move to another location, as no doubt wherever Sam had gone, it would result in a lot of cops, soldiers and guns coming their way. So in the back of the army truck and Bedford they moved back through the gates, with Adam locking the gates after them. They then quickly relocated to the Robotics and General Engineering building that Katie had full access too.

As they jumped out of the trucks, and started heading into their new hiding place, Adam spoke to Thomas.

"Man, I need to get to Trish! Damn it, look at the time its a quarter to seven, I told her I would be home by four to give her a lift back to the hospital Thomas."

Adam checked his mobile phone, and sure enough he had several missed calls. He had turned it off earlier when they were searching in the bush, as he feared its ringing would alert whoever was near.

"Make sure these guys all get into the building safely, and that cart with the lead box is secured somewhere safe too. I'm going to stay out here for a few minutes and call Trish, she will be worried sick."

"Ok Adam, you do what you need to do man, go see her if you need to, we will be fine. They won't think about looking here, if they look at all," Thomas told him, concerned for Trish himself.

As Richie, the last to enter the building, pulled the cart behind him and through the door, Adam dialed Trish's number.

"Adam!"

"Trish! Honey, I'm so sorry."

"Where are you, are you ok? I was so worried!" Trish told him.

She was still sitting in an empty waiting room, having processed through the only two patients who had arrived since she started her shift. One being an elderly gentleman who had fallen and broken his wrist, after a few sherries too many. "Darling, the World's coming to an end, so I want to leave it with a smile on my face, and a blur in my eyes so I can't see whatever evil is coming for us" he told her. The other patient being a Police Officer who had tripped on a curb while running after some looters of a small grocery store, and gashed his head open.

"Any reason to steal, and the scum come out of the woodwork, and take advantage of other peoples circumstances," he told Trish as she put a temporary dressing on his wound until it could be stitched.

Adam tried to reassure Trish best he could. "I'm fine, we have met some, well, some interesting people alright. I'll tell you when I get home, it's way too unbelievable to even try and describe over the phone. So, you got to work ok?"

"Yeah, Donna gave me a lift. There's a curfew on through the whole city babe! Be careful, ok?"

"Yeah, of course. What time will you be home Trish?"

"We finish shift at 1am, so I should be home by 1.20? Will you be home then, please?"

"I'll make sure I am Honey. Trish ... I love you so much, my heart aches to see your face, to look into your eyes, and to feel your lips against mine." Adam almost broke down, his emotional state had been tested all day, especially since killing the robed man earlier.

"I miss you too, you are my life Adam, don't ever leave me. Hey, I need to see to a patient who's just arrived, call me later, you promise?"

"I will. Be safe."

Adam hung up. He turned and walked through the large glass doors to join the others in the four story University building that was full of labs, lecture rooms, and offices. Just as the glass door shut behind him, he thought he detected a sudden bright light from outside, so he stepped back through the door, and cautiously looked around.

Not finding anything unusual, he again turned to re-enter the building, when again there was a sudden burst of light, not blinding, nor like a spotlight, but more like a strong glow, like the light enveloping the path under a streetlight. He looked up and saw where the light source was coming from, it was from a bright yellow orb of light passing overhead, maybe 100 metres up, fast, but not as fast as a jet plane. He thought at first it must be a helicopter, with a searchlight, maybe the Police looking for him and his newly formed gang of refugees, refugees that were attempting to flee chaos in search of order. But there were no helicopter sounds; no thrumming of the blades or loud explosions of its pistons from the engine, there was only silence. Within five seconds it had passed overhead, and disappeared into some low cloud.

Adam noticed that he didn't feel the slightest bit surprised at all after witnessing this unusual sight. It was as if his ability to feel surprised or bewildered had been so numbed by the day's events so far; nothing could surprise or shock him again. After a minute or so looking into the clouds, expecting maybe a three headed dragon, or a group of flying fluorescent pink pigs to suddenly appear, he entered the building and tracked down where the group had located itself for now.

"Hey, you guys did say you weren't from another planet huh?" Adam said as he entered the lecture hall they were now all sitting in, "So, you really sure about that? Sure you didn't arrive on a spaceship or anything, like the one that just went past a moment ago?"

"What are you talking about?" Edotha asked, looking concerned.

"I just saw a bright, um, well ... a bright something fly overhead, and it wasn't a plane, and it wasn't a helicopter, so that sort of leaves spaceships," Adam replied.

Suddenly the robed seven looked unsettled, Eo stood, looked at Edotha, then Adam.

"It's the Elite, they too must know the haze has gone, and they are surveying the city, they will come, within a few days. You have got to warn your people!" Eo told them, looking anxious, and deadly serious.

# CHAPTER TWENTYTHREE

Di was intrigued by the samples she had collected.

Since Henry and her had found Adam and Tricia, and the crashed Police Car at the end of the Northern highway, she had been thinking about what they had seen. The huge Redwood trees, the mature bushes, and the difference in temperature, all of these discoveries intrigued her yet annoyed her in that she couldn't understand how they could all be connected, yet must be.

Di had returned to the field at the end of the highway the day after the initial meeting and experience, and had spent almost all of that day there. Though two soldiers now guarded the end of the highway to prevent anyone leaving and entering by road, they had allowed her to pass. Partially due to her explaining her qualifications in horticulture and how they related to the 'weirdness', which was what many in the city had now termed the strange events, but probably more because she knew how to get to any man's heart, with her beautiful smile, a flick of her long silky blonde hair, and a few flutters of her luscious eyelashes. It was unfortunate for the two male soldiers that Di was actually more interested in her own gender than theirs, but this was not a fact that was their business to know.

After collecting many cuttings, bark scrapings, and dozens of photos on her digital camera, she loaded up her silver 2009 Subaru Impreza, and headed back down the highway, giving a friendly wave to the soldiers as she passed back through their roadblock.

She decided she would call in and say hi to Jack and his sister who lived not much farther down the highway, remembering the driveway to their house from Jack's description the day before. As she drove into the driveway she noticed the gates to the two main paddocks were wide open, and there were four goats she could see wondering around unfenced and untethered. This struck her as odd, as the first rule of any farm is to have the gates closed at all times. However, she thought they were probably just moving stock, or horses, or maybe they didn't worry about closing the gates on their small lot.

She rang the doorbell several times, despite the front door being ajar.

She called out "Jack, hello? Anyone home?" There was no answer.

Di entered the house, hesitating, knowing that she may give the elderly couple a fright if they suddenly rounded the corner and saw someone they weren't expecting in their house. She had walked just a few metres from the front when she saw the drips of blood on the carpet.

"Hello, is everyone ok? Has someone had an accident?" She was worried, and starting to feel a little frightened.

She rounded the corner of the curved hallway, and entered the kitchen. She saw Jack's body immediately, and screamed. She frantically looked around, and noticed the fridge door was open, some food was lying on the floor, and the fridge shelves were almost completely empty. Someone had obviously ransacked it. Di staggered in shock through the kitchen and into the lounge, where she then saw Susan's body, she shuddered and sobbed loudly, mainly from the fear of not knowing what was going on, who had done this, and why.

Di remembered what her partner once told her.

"Fear is an odd, yet so powerful emotion. It seems to begin with just an inkling of the unknown. It grows as the possibilities that explain that unknown factor begin to come into our mind; could it be this, could it be that, or could it be something we have never come across before. If you do not face the fear head on, and determine the reason behind the unknown and beat it back to where it began, it starts to grip you, take over every thought, until even being able to breathe becomes a conscious effort, and every drop of sweat that starts to drip, feels like a chip of ice sliding down a nerve."

Di thought about those words, but then quickly decided the only safe thing to do was run! She ran through the house, taking a wide berth around Susan's body as though she feared one of the corpses arms would suddenly reach out at her, the pale lifeless hand suddenly surging with energy and grabbing her ankle. She left the lounge, gripping the doorframe to steady herself, as her ability to balance seemed to have run away ahead of her in its own flight from fear. As she ran down the hallway, she heard a male voice shout behind her.

"Get her! Stop her! Jondiso, grab her!"

She ran faster, almost tripping over her own feet. Her heart beat harder, faster, she could feel it hitting her ribs at every beat as if it was fighting with another entity within her own chest. Her breath was hot, feeling like air from a furnace as each breath left her mouth, her body aching, pleading for oxygen to feed her muscles that were working at double speed. She ran through the front doorway, and as she ran towards her car, she heard another two voices.

"Stop or die!"

"Jondiso, take her down!"

Di reached her car, and as she flung the drivers door open something hit her left arm, tearing the flesh, the object then made a metallic sound as it hit the window of the car's rear door, ricocheting onto the ground.

"A spear? What the hell?" Di said to herself as she struggled to get into the drivers seat, her arm protesting with pain and throbbing as blood poured from it.

She locked all the car doors at once, using the central locking switch on her driver side door. She pulled the car keys from her white nylon jacket pocket with her right hand, fumbling as she tried to get them into the ignition, and as they slid in there was a massive thud in front of her. She screamed as a man's body landed on the bonnet. His face then suddenly appeared in front of her, glaring at her through the windscreen, hate in his eyes, hands flat against the glass which he then started to hit incredibly hard.

"Get out bitch! Get out of the vehicle now you Elite filth!" The man's voice, though muffled through the toughened glass, was so full of aggression and vengeance it seemed to almost pierce Di's ears, and made her wince with every word shouted towards her.

She turned the key, then having to use her right hand, reached across to the gearshift lever and put the car into reverse. She then slammed her foot on the accelerator, trying to adequately judge the clutch pedal, as she put her right hand back on the steering wheel, her left arm hanging limply as any attempt to lift it resulted in horrendous stabbing pains shooting up her arm and into her shoulder.

The wild man, half on the bonnet and half on the windscreen slid off almost instantly, shouting curses at her as he did. He hit the ground and rolled several times, ending up against the paddock fence.

Di kept the car reversing until she was eventually back out on the highway, and with pain, and blood now covering much of the gear shift and gap between the front seats, she managed to get the lever to shift straight into second gear, and off she sped, swerving like a crazy drunk driver as she stumbled shifting up gears until she was in fifth.

One handed steering, both feet pressed hard, one on the other against the accelerator peddle, and eyes stinging with tears, Di escaped the mad man, the corpses, and the farm, yet she couldn't escape the fear that still filled her mind and her heart. She screamed, she sobbed, she swore, and she yearned to be in the arms of her partner Rachel who waited for her at home, back in Duntoon, the city that was once in the year 2012, yet unbeknown to Di had somehow been thrust into the year of 2367.

# CHAPTER TWENTYFOUR

**'Duntoon TV advises viewers the following is an emergency broadcast, also broadcast live on all local radio stations. Following, is an emergency announcement by the Mayor of Duntoon, Honorable Peter Green.'** The TV in the hospital waiting room had been turned to almost full volume, as many of the hospital staff believed, or more-so hoped, that somehow this message would sort everything out, as long as they heard it nice and loud. Tricia sat next to her good friend Donna in the Waiting room, ready to triage anyone who arrived during the Mayor's announcement.


**'Citizens of Duntoon, I speak to you on this night of the 29th March, of the year 2012, in the hope that I can put your minds at rest as much as is possible, and inform you of the situation we find ourselves in. However, I fear that what I am about to inform you of will not fulfill my desire to support your need for hope, and may not fulfill mine or that of my councilors.'**


**'The Manager of Duntoon City Council, Mrs Alexandria Hastings and myself, have decided that the city of Duntoon is now under a 48 hour curfew, where only emergency personnel, and essential council personnel are permitted to travel around the city, and only on official business.'**


"Yeah, tell us something we don't know you twit!" Donna said, inpatient as to hearing what everyone really wanted to know.


**'It appears that as of the early morning of the 28th March, 2012, the area surrounding Duntoon suffered some type of traumatic event, an event of such scale and mystery that we can not begin to conceive any idea of what has occurred. All communications with anyone anywhere outside of an area approximately 10 kilometres either side of central Duntoon, are no longer possible. We do not know why, nor when they can be reconnected. The highways ...'**

The Mayor paused, and was seen to shuffle his feet nervously as he stood at the front of the Duntoon City Council Building, in its lighted foyer. **'The highways ... in and out of Duntoon are no longer usable, and we are not sure when they will be in the future. The airport is closed, and all bus services have ceased until further notice'**

"Highways are not usable! Are you kidding me?' Tricia shouted at the TV, much to the astonishment of the small crowd in the Waiting Room who had also gathered there to hear the Mayor's announcement. "They don't exist any more! They have been replaced with trees, bush, grass ..." She suddenly realised people were staring at her, some appeared terrified by what she was saying, others appeared worried that she had just lost her grasp on reality. She stopped speaking.

**'As I stated before, the City of Duntoon is under a compulsory 48-hour curfew, with the exception of emergency personnel and essential council officials. You must stay at your place of residence and do not leave your property, awaiting a further announcement from myself at 7pm on the 31st March. If you have an emergency, call 111, as the City phone lines are still working. Outside power sources however have been lost, yet we are lucky to have our own hydro power station within the city limits, and after a small hitch earlier today, it has been repaired and will be back online and power will be fully restored. This should occur within four hours, and this message will be repeated then when everyone has access to television, rather than just the few of you using battery or emergency generator power. It will be repeated every 30 minutes until 7pm on the 31st March when I hope to bring you more enlightening and encouraging information of what has occurred, and what the next few days and weeks will bring."**

**'Lastly, the city of Duntoon is now under Martial law.'**

People watching with Trish and Donna gasped, Tricia grabbed one of Donna's hands, and they held each other tightly.

'People not obeying military or police officials, may be arrested, or if decisively contemptuous of the directions being given by officials, may be shot. I repeat, the city of Duntoon is now under Martial law, People not obeying military or police officials, may be arrested, or shot.' The Mayor now stared directly into the camera. 'This is the end of my announcement. May God look down on us all in Duntoon, and be merciful to us.'

There was silence in the Waiting room, other than one young student nurse, who cried quietly, comforted by an elderly cleaning lady who placed her arm around the nurse's shoulder.

"It's ok, everything will be ok dear," Though she spoke reassuringly, her eyes betrayed her, and they gave the message that the World was now a frightening and dangerous place to be a part of.

-----------------------------------------

The others in the group watched and listened as Adam spoke to someone on his mobile phone after answering a call. He had spoken with love in his voice, so it was obvious he was speaking to his wife Trish. But the words he then started using, "Oh, you are kidding", "No way, that's crazy!" had given all of the eavesdroppers the impression that something was very, very wrong.

Adam said his farewell to his Wife, told her again how much he loved her and then promised to see her later that night. It was 7.45pm. Adam flipped his red Samsung phone shut, and slid it into his jacket pocket. He stared at the ground for a moment, then faced the group who still sat in the lecture hall looking like students who had turned up to a promised student party, only to find there was no alcohol and no party, and instead there was a lecture about how things in life can change in an instant.

"Looks like you guys will need to be housed here for a while, because there's no way we can get seven people in weird clothes like yours through armed road blocks, especially when the whole town is under curfew."

Henry stood up, looking shocked.

"What? You pulling my leg young fella? A curfew, what a Pakaru sort of a thing to do to a city already on tender-hooks. Let me guess, the dumb ass mayor and the city manager are behind all this, huh?"

"Looks like it Henry," Adam replied. He then looked at Katie, then Edotha. "Can I talk to you two outside for a minute?"

Edotha glanced at the other female of their group who nodded her head. Katie and her then agreed and walked out with Adam into the corridor that connected the different lecture halls and offices.

"Edotha, tell me and Katie more about these lights in the sky. Eo said the Elite will be coming, and to warn our people? What does he mean?" Adam asked.

"The lights are aircraft the Elite use when they are hunting us."

"Hunting you?" Katie said, sounding astounded by what Edotha had just said.

"Yes, hunting us. If any of the Denees, that's what they call us, 'Denees', have attempted to attack one of their cities, trying to get food, medical supplies or to enable one of our Eo's to upload information, they come after us, and usually kill whoever they find."

"Wow, that contained so many pieces of information that are completely over my head, it's not funny." Katie told her. "Right, one thing at a time. Why are you called 'Denees?"

"I don't know, we have just always been called that by the Elite. We all have our own tribal names, depending on which tribe you are with, which is determined geographically. We are from the West side of the South Island, and are mostly peaceful, unless we have to fight in self defense."

"Huh!" Adam interjected, "Peaceful? You killed two cops, and attempted to kill Sam as well, and were going to kill us earlier on!"

"No! You don't understand, we were defending ourselves, the Elite can kill you within seconds, their weapons are hundreds of times superior to ours, and to yours from what I have seen,"

"Go on Edotha, about the name 'Denees', please," Katie restated, trying to calm things back down.

"As I said, I do not know. Eo may know, or he may need to get an upload of history information in more detail than the basics he has."

Katie continued her questions. "Ok, so what about the aircraft? What sort of aircraft makes no noise?"

"The Elite use fragments of CMQ, Crystal Mountain Quartz, to power their craft. They only seat a maximum of six people, and use a type of magnetic force-field to travel through the air. Eo may be able to give you more details, but he explained it to me by using the analogy of a magnet with a negative poll pushing against one with a positive poll."

"Ok well maybe we can get our heads around all that later," Katie said, looking even more puzzled.

"Why would the Elite, be coming here, after us?" Adam asked.

"Because you are not them, and you are something they did not know existed until now. Their response to anything they don't understand is to destroy it. Besides, you have CMQ, and lots of it, it is priceless to them and they will want it, and they are used to getting what they want."

"Sound like nice people" Katie replied, sarcastically.

"Oh, no, they are definitely not nice." Edotha answered, sadness was evident in her eyes.

# CHAPTER TWENTYFIVE

Tricia jumped in surprise at the sight and sound of four soldiers rushing through the Emergency Department doors, two of them carrying a woman who was obviously suffering some type of serious injury as a lot of blood was visible on her clothing, and she was barely conscious.

"Bring her straight through," Tricia advised the soldiers as they neared her open plan triage office, "That's it, straight into the Department, into Resus. Two. What happened to her?"

"We aren't sure; she drove into our roadblock, literally! Hit the side of our truck, luckily at pretty low speed. Looked like she was only just with it, you know, only just conscious," the tallest of the four soldiers replied.

"She has an open wound injury to her arm, she may have been shot, possibly stabbed."

As the soldiers laid her gently onto the hospital bed in the resuscitation room, Trish saw the victims face clearly.

"I know this lady, her name's Di. I met her yesterday on the, the highway. She is a civil engineer, or something like that, came out there with a guy called Henry to look at the highway ..." She paused, trying to think of an appropriate adjective, "problem."

Trish was surprised and saddened to have her second meeting with Di in circumstances such as these. She examined her arm, and noted the flesh and muscle had been exposed in a nasty wound.

"Looks like she will need surgery, possibly a skin graft to repair this."

Trish recorded Di's vital signs, blood pressure, heart rate, respirations, and placed an oxygen mask on her face. As she did, Di stirred.

"Tricia? Are you an angel?" Di muttered, her eyes watering, and her face as pale as a cloud.

Trish smiled down at her. "No Di, I'm not an angel sweetie, but I am a nurse, and you are in hospital now, its ok, we will get you fixed up."

Three of the soldiers left the room, and made their way to the waiting room, to wait for their colleague who remained behind, the one who had spoken to Trish earlier. Trish made Di as comfortable as she could, and tucked a thin hospital blanket over her after removing her shoes and socks.

"Hospital?" Di asked, her words only barely audible.

"Yes Di, in Duntoon hospital, its ok sweetheart, just rest, the Doctor will be here shortly," Trish reassured her.

"Hospital! Jack and Susan, dead, DEAD! Trish, someone killed Jack and Susan!"

"Shush sweetie, it's ok. No one has killed Jack and Susan honey, it was just a bad dream, because you have lost a lot of blood, just relax." Tricia smoothed Di's hair back over her head and off of her face. But Di didn't settle, she became more and more anxious.

"No, no dream, they tried to kill me too, threw a spear at me Trish, a spear! My arm, I thought I had got away!"

"Come on Di, you are safe now, calm down□"  Trish again tried to quiet Di, worried her anxious state may result in her losing even more blood as she started to try and sit up.

"You need to relax Di, I need to get an IV into you."

"No, no, I thought I had got away, but they were on the highway, on horses, on foot, ducking and diving on and off the highway when they saw my car! They are coming

Trish, they are only a few kilometres away, and they are coming!" Di blacked out from a loss of blood, or maybe from a hefty dose of fear.

-------------------------------------------------

Adam explained to the group as a whole that he needed to get home to his Wife Trish as he had promised her. Henry and Thomas also needed to do the same. He, with the help of Edotha and Katie, explained that the city was under Marshall law, meaning they would all be at risk if they tried to leave the building as a group. Adam assured them that he believed they would be safe from Sam and the Police, as it was unlikely they would find them holed up in the building they were in, as it was one of 40 different University buildings, with many stories in each building that they could be in. Katie, along with her two less esteemed side kicks, Larry and Richie, agreed to stay with the group of robed ones, or 'Denees' as they were apparently known by the Elite, and they would raid the staff cafeteria to ensure they were all well fed.

As a group they agreed that Adam, Thomas, and Henry would meet them in the morning at 6.30am, and plan on how they would transport them back to where they had originally found them, with a stop at the Council Chambers on the way to warn the Mayor of the danger that the Elite now posed.

"It's best if we travel together," Adam told Henry and Thomas as they walked outside the robotics and engineering building that had become a temporary home to the 'Denees'. "If we have to explain ourselves to armed soldiers and cops, I think it is best we do it all together."

"Yes, I think you are right Adam, Henry - you with us?" Thomas asked his aged new friend.

"Well, you young fella's know best," Henry answered with a smile.

They left the University campus in the Getz. A rather strange sight, three large and muscle bound men in a small car, traveling through a deserted city near midnight, but in these days that had come about so quickly, nothing appeared very odd at all any more.

"Ok, guys just relax, and let me see if I can talk our way through this," Adam told his two passengers, now friends, as they neared a roadblock.

As they pulled up five metres or so from an army truck parked across the main oneway route south, they could not see where the guards had positioned themselves. So Adam climbed out of the car, with his arms raised to ensure they knew he wasn't armed.

"Hello? We just want to get back to our homes in South Duntoon. We have been doing some maintenance work at the University, only just heard there is a curfew in place. Hello?" Adam shouted out, but with no reply.

Adam slowly and cautiously walked forward towards the Army truck. He heard sounds behind him and turned to see Henry and Thomas were getting out of the car, following Adam's lead with their arms raised.

"What are you blokes doing?" Adam asked, sounding alarmed.

"Not letting you face these guys alone Adam." Thomas told him. "We are in this together my friend."

Adam looked Thomas in the eyes, then Henry, and smiled. "Thanks."

Adam believed that in modern times money and pride seemed to have become the best friends of man, and it was rare to see or experience true camaraderie. It is all too common to only see it when men are faced with tragedy, or circumstances where they share life and death experiences on an everyday basis, such as those who give their lives following the orders of war-worshiping politicians, and psychotic religious leaders hell-bent on pushing their beliefs onto everyone, or death onto those who do not blindly follow. Adam, Henry and Thomas had become true comrades after experiencing the ultimate emotion, that of desperation to see the ones they loved.

They walked in unison to the army truck, still calling out "Hello, any one there?", yet with no reply. As they walked around the truck they came across three dead bodies, soldiers, all suffering head injuries, two with arrows protruding from their foreheads.

"Oh my good Lord, what has happened? The Elite?" Henry asked.

"Must be, poor souls," Thomas replied, shaking his head.

"No. No this is not from the Elite, this is from Denees!" Adam told them, as he walked over and retrieved an automatic weapon from one of the now lifeless military men. "Denees! We've been conned!"

The three men rushed back to the car, turned around and sped back to the University buildings. Within a few minutes they were pulling up outside the Robotics and Engineering building where the group was housed inside.

Adam and Thomas burst through the doors, while Henry, not wanting a confrontation, waited out in the corridor.

"You murderers!" Adam shouted as he entered the lecture room the group still sat in. Staring at Edotha and Eo in particular he continued, "Your lot have killed more people, soldiers this time! I thought you only killed in self defense, like hell!"

They looked at Adam, seemingly shocked at what he was saying.

"What are you talking about, we haven't left this room," Eo replied as he stood and confronted Adam by walking over to him, and staring him in the face.

"Yeah, well there are obviously a lot more of you, and now they are wondering around our city killing whoever they come across! We just found three soldiers, dead, two with crossbow arrows in them, the other looked like he had been stabbed. The arrows were made of that weird metal you 'Denees' use. Explain that!"

Eo turned and looked at Edotha. She looked down at the ground, but said nothing. Eo walked back to his chair and sat down.

"Adam, calm down," Katie pleaded, worrying that the situation may turn violent.

"Yeah Dude, just chill. You can't blame these guys for something they didn't do man," Larry added.

"What? You have nothing to say now?" Adam asked the group, seemingly ignoring what Katie and Larry had said. "You are just going to sit there, and say nothing huh? Well, I say we call the cops ourselves, and they can get what information they need out of you if it is going to stop more people being killed."

"Adam. How do you know it wasn't those Elite folk who Eo warned us were coming? He said they were dangerous," Katie asked, walking over to him.

"No Katie," Thomas answered, "Adam is right. It looked like the results of the same type of weapons as these guys were going to use against us earlier today. I don't think a highly advanced group like the Elite apparently are would be using crossbows."

"He's right," Edotha suddenly said. "It would have been Denees, but not from our area. I am pretty sure it will be the northern Denees. They are very aggressive; they have killed many of us from the West over the last few years. They take our food, destroy our homes, and have even taken one of our other Eo's so they could get information they needed."

Adam, Thomas and Katie stared at Edotha, not quite knowing what to say. Larry and Rich looked at each other, as if they were enjoying watching a sci fi movie together, looks of excitement but confusion on their faces.

They then all startled at the sudden shouting from Henry out in the corridor, as they turned towards the door six armed Police came through the doors, followed by Sam.

"Don't any of you move! Now we will get some justice!" Sam said, with a grin of self-satisfaction on his face.

# CHAPTER TWENTYSIX

"You, the freaks in the robes, come with us," Sam ordered.

"Where are you taking them Sam?" Adam asked.

"The Police Station, where we can deal with the ones who killed my colleagues, my friends."

"I hope you are going to go through the proper systems Sam, ensure they have representation, a court trial, and ..."

Sam interrupted Adam, "This city is now under martial law, the Mayor and the City Manager will decide what happens to them, not a court. Right, move it!" He signaled to Edotha, Eo and the others in the group to leave the room.

They stood, and left as one, Edotha making only brief eye contact with Adam as they left, but he noticed a look of calm in her eyes, like she was ok with what Sam was doing.

"What about us, you going to treat us like crap as well?" Henry suddenly challenged Sam, walking into the room from the corridor where he had still been standing until now.

"I have no qualms with you. You can all make your way home, I'll make sure the patrols know to let you through the roadblocks."

"But the roadblock ..." Thomas started to say, when he was interrupted by Adam.

"The roadblock will be no problem now Thomas, you heard Sam, he's going to let them all know." Adam glared at Thomas, obviously wanting him to shut the heck up.

"Oh yeah, oh great, thanks Sam," Thomas stuttered.

"Yeah, well, ok. So, you guys all ok? Who are you Miss?" Sam looked at Katie.

"I'm a Professor here at the University, and yes we are all fine." As she spoke she glanced at Larry and Richie, who had both moved their chairs to hide the trolley with the trap that contained the crystals.

"Right. Well, I'll catch up with you Adam, another day," Sam told Adam, face to face as he walked from the room.

Adam had the feeling that Sam had some unfinished business with him, yet this wasn't the time or place to finish that business.

Katie accompanied Adam outside to watch as the two Police paddy wagons left with the Denees inside them. The other four had stayed back in the room, now without the Denees present, they no doubt wanted to try and come to terms with the strange events of the last few hours, without part of the strangeness being present.

"Do you think they will be ok?" Katie said to Adam as the last Police vehicle left their sight.

"I don't know, but I hope so. Sam is one crazy cop though, crazy with vengeance burning a hole in his heart. Little does he know trying to fill that hole with more death, will only turn the hole into a rip that can't be fixed." Adam appeared to be talking more to himself, than replying to Katie as he remembered the life he had taken that morning, and could feel the rip that now existed in his own heart.

"Surely he can't just go killing six people in cold blood, the other officers wouldn't let him, would they?"

"No, I guess not. There are actually seven of them you know, poor guys," Adam replied.

"No, no there was only six that left with the Police, I counted them as they climbed into the Police vans."

"Are you sure?"

"Yip, I'm positive."

They rushed back into the building, and into the Lecture room. There they were greeted by a smiling Larry, Richie, Thomas, Henry, and one young, very slim, and rather frightened looking brunette haired female Denee.

"What the heck!" Adam exclaimed.

"Dude! She was sitting on the trolley man, me and Richie made sure those pricks didn't see her," Larry answered, with pride in his voice.

"Well done boys!" Katie said with a smile, "At least you have done one thing right today. What's your name sweetie?"

"Amberley," she answered, "I am Princess Amberley."

"Wow, score!" Richie shouted, giving Larry a high five.

"So that's why Edotha seemed ok with it, and they all left so readily. To protect their, their Princess," Adam remarked to his friends, who seemed excited to have become the new Royal Minders.

-----------------------------------------

Donna dropped Tricia off at her home, where Tricia hoped to soon see Adam again after almost a whole day since last seeing him. On the trip from the hospital to Tricia and Adam's place they had traveled through two roadblocks, one on the one way system back out of town, guarded by two soldiers, the other by a lone Police Officer on the main intersection.

"Are you going to be ok Trish, home alone until Adam gets here," asked a worried Donna.

"Yes, I'll be fine, I think. It's just mind blowing really, this weirdness that seems to have overtaken everything. No way in or out of town, talk of UFOs, martial law, and now Di saying Jack and Susan have been murdered. I just can't get my head around it all."

"You are telling me. But, maybe it's just the next phase of life, you know what I mean? Maybe, like all changes we face, this is the ultimate one that we are just going to have to come to terms with, somehow."

"Yeah, I suppose we have no choice really. My Mum always said, I mean says, life is like painting a work of art. For each of us it's different, and sometimes what appears on your canvas is a surprise even to you, but it's all about how you work at getting it back to what you wanted, the more effort and enjoyment, the better the end result."

"Your Mum is a wise lady Trish, just like you, and I am sure one day you will be reunited with her," Donna replied, seeing the sadness on Tricia's face as she spoke of her Mother, who she never ended up visiting at the campground because of the highway's sudden end, and now Tricia wondered whether even the campground still existed.

Donna drove off after seeing Tricia enter the house, and lock the door behind her as Donna had insisted she do "and double check it!"

It wasn't until 1.15am when Adam drove into their driveway. Tricia's eyes lit up when she saw him through the living room window, getting out of her car. Her heart suddenly felt lighter, and the air clearer. True love is a remedy to cure any heartache. If only temporarily it is a respite that we all need at times, and for Tricia this was definitely one of those times.

"Sweetheart, I missed you so much," Adam told Trish as they wrapped their arms around each other after Tricia opened the door for him, before he even had a chance to get the key out of his jacket pocket.

"Adam, it's just been so crazy!"

"Oh yeah. Let me sum up my night. Time travel, some mystery crystals that could power a country, dead soldiers, cops, paddy wagons, lights in the sky and a Princess - beat that honey!" Adam laughed, yet absent was the usual mandatory smile that accompanied most laughter. Adam didn't know what emotion he was feeling, as it seemed the World around him was beyond normal emotions.

"Do you remember the woman who was with Henry when we first met them, out at the end of the highway? You know, that pretty blonde - Di?"

"Yeah of course, how could I forget her?" Adam said with a smirk on his face, which quickly disappeared when Trish glared at him.

"I mean, um, we waited together for Henry to come back and get us, so I got to know her a little." Trish glared at him even more intensely.

"Um, you know what I mean! We talked about our lives and boring stuff like that."

"Well." Trish hesitated, and then continued with a slight sour note to her voice, though that quickly disappeared as she spoke. "She was brought into the ER, she had been attacked - a spear she said."

"Oh no! Is she ok?"

"Yes, she'll be fine, but she told me that Jack and his sister Susan have been murdered."

"Jack and Susan?" Adam asked, not sure if he knew who she was talking about.

"Yes, you know, the old guy who arrived in the Bedford, almost crashed it off the highway. Susan was his sister."

"Oh yeah! Murdered? More death, what the heck! A spear – damn, I bet I can guess who will be responsible for that."

"More death?" Di asked, looking concerned.

"We came across three soldiers, all dead at a roadblock not far from the University. We think the Denees, you know - the ones in robes I told you about on the phone, we think they killed them. But not the ones we had with us, apparently these ones come from the North, aggressive murdering scumbags by the sounds of what we were told."

"Oh no, that's what Di was saying, that they were coming, and they had weapons and things. You think we are in danger?"

"Well honey, from now on, I'm not letting you out of my sight. Where I go, you go, and where you go - I will follow, to the end of the Earth if I have to."

Adam and Trish cuddled for a few minutes in the Living room, walking off to bed, hand in hand, wondering what the new morning would bring to the under siege City of Duntoon.

# CHAPTER TWENTYSEVEN

A high pitch sound, on, off, on, off. It was ringing in Adam's head, or was it the whole room, or the whole World? Could this be the one last traumatic event that would see the entire Earth, as Adam and Trish had always known it, come to an end? The sound was piercing, as if it was designed to grasp you within its volume, shake your bones, and enter your very soul.

Adam opened his eyes, blinked a few times, looking at Trish laying next to him, he realized he had been sleeping, dreaming - yet the high pitch sounds continued, over and over.

"Man I'm stupid," he mumbled as he reached over to the digital alarm clock on the bedside table next to him, and hit the snooze button. "Trish, you awake babe? Damn, who set the alarm for 7am, need to sleep, so tired."

"No, asleep, quiet," Trish mumbled back at him, eyes still closed, and pulling the bed covers over her head.

"Maybe it was all a dream, just a bad frigging dream," Adam thought to himself, hoping if that was what he believed, it would be so. He lay back down, snuggled up to Trish and closed his eyes, soon drifting off to a dream world full of amazing silent aircraft, ominous figures in robes marching up and down the street, and glowing crystals attached to power poles. Then he heard Edotha's voice.

"Adam, Adam ... we need you Adam."

Then Henry's voice "Wake up fella, we need to get a move on my friend!"

Lastly there was Eo's voice.

"WAKE UP ADAM ... NOW!"

"What the heck!" Adam, sat straight up in bed, opened his eyes and to his surprise there was Edotha, Henry, and Eo standing beside their bed. "What the heck are you guys doing here, in my room? Edotha, Eo, you were under arrest, how'd you get away?"

Trish woke, and sat up, looking shocked and frightened at the site of three people standing next to their bed, two of them complete strangers, though she recognised Henry.

"Adam? What's this all about," Trish asked, wrapping her arm around his.

"It's ok Trish. Edotha, Eo, this is my Wife Tricia. Tricia, this is Edotha and Eo."

"Um, yeah, nice to meet you, but how did you get into our house?" Trish asked as she rubbed her eyes.

"You think that primitive locking device can keep anyone out?" Eo answered. "I picked the lock in an instant."

"He did. It was a sight to see let me tell you. He took a fine piece of copper wire, or looked like that, out of his pocket, then a second or two later your door was wide open," Henry told them, with a big smile on his face, patting Eo on the back.

"Ok, but why, and how did these two get away from the cops, and meet up with you?" Adam asked, wondering whether in fact he was still dreaming.

"The Police vehicles were ambushed by the Northern Denees," Eo told them. "They set a trap, two of them laid across the road, like they had been injured, the police vehicles stopped. As soon as they got out, a dozen or so others jumped in the cabs. Many of the Police were killed, but some were able to escape. The Northerns, they asked us to join them. We told them we would, so they would release us, but as soon as we had the chance we left them and ran back to where we had last seen you."

"At the University?" Adam asked.

"Yes," Edotha answered, and took over from Eo, explaining their morning so far.

"When we joined with Henry, Thomas, Katie and the other two, we rejoiced at seeing Princess Amberley was ok. We owe you our lives for keeping her safe."

"They told us," said Henry "that they must meet with the Mayor, and explain the danger that the City is in, not just from the Northern Denees, but from those other folk, the Elites?"

"Yes, the Elites." Edotha answered.

"So why didn't you guys just take them straight to the Mayor, why come here Henry?" Adam asked, still puzzled by the need for the bedroom invasion.

"Because, you are our leader Adam, we need you to lead us to the Mayor, and to help your city defend itself from the Elite," Edotha answered.

"What?" Adam said. "Um, eh? Your leader? Why on Earth do you think I should be your leader?"

Henry walked over to Adam, and sat on the side of his bed.

"Adam, my good friend, at times of war, and during times when a people face desperation, they need leadership. They need leadership from someone who can keep a cool head, make decisions that incorporate looking after all those around them. You, Adam, in the last couple of days have shown you have all those qualities and more. The Denees need you, and I believe this whole city needs you."

"They are right," Trish agreed, smiling with pride and love for the man who sat next to her, her husband. "You are the one person who can get us all through the unknown that we now face Adam. On this day Adam, our wedding anniversary, which I know must have slipped your mind, and it's no wonder it has, I give you the gift of my never-ending support and love for the days, weeks, months and, I hope, years to come." She leant over to him, and kissed him on the cheek.

"Right then," Adam said, "If I'm going to lead thousands of people into the future, I better change out of these PJ's! Oh, and Trish, happy anniversary Honey, I didn't forget. Today we were supposed to still be at the campground, where I had arranged a bouquet of flowers to be delivered to you first thing this morning, along with a string quartet to play to you while I cooked a BBQ in the evening. Instead, please accept my whole hearted promise of a love for you that will never die."

Trish and Adam kissed again, and the others left the room to give them some privacy while they dressed.

"Darn, it's so cold!" Trish said as she changed out of her nightie.

"Cold, damn it, look at the temperature gauge on the wall, its ten degrees below what it usually is this time of year!" Adam replied, shivering.

# CHAPTER TWENTYEIGHT

The other five Denees had stayed back at the University Campus, having changed buildings in case the Police came back there looking for them. Henry, Edotha and Eo had traveled together in Henry's truck, having had Edotha and Eo change into more readily accepted clothing before they left. The Fashion Design School, a new department of the University, had proved a good addition after all, despite the many objections from the very arrogant and academic academia.

Meeting in Adam and Trish's Living Room, the group of five decided to come up with a structured plan of how they would attack the day, rather than take risks which might see them end up like the Police escort the night before.

"One question I have," Adam said, "Is how did you lot get through the roadblocks?"

Henry shook his head. "There were only two between the campus and here, no doubt you passed them last night, including the one with the dead soldiers?"

"Yes, we did, but the second one had a Police Officer and two soldiers. It took us two a fair bit of convincing we were merely two hospital workers going back home before they let us through."

"Yeah, well, I am afraid Adam that when we reached that one, it was abandoned, though there were some blood stains on the road."

"How can these Northern Denees fight armed professionals and win, when they just have primitive weapons?" Adam looked defeated, as though the mysteries that seemed to infiltrate every part of their new life, were just too much for him to keep on accepting.

"Primitive? Are you joking? Our weapons are made from the most modern alloys that we have taken from the Elites over many years, and then crafted with our own machinery. Not primitive at all, one of our spears can fly up to 80 metres, and still kill cattle or Shaybons," Eo answered.

"Ok, a few more questions. Firstly, why don't you just use guns like us, or the amazing weapons you say the Elites have? Secondly, what the heck are Shaybons? Lastly, how do you run machinery if you have no electricity?" Adam asked, trying not to sound ignorant.

"Your guns use some type of explosive powder. Explosive powders were banned in the Shameful Years, around 2020 - 2045. Shaybons. You don't know what Shaybons are?" Eo laughed, "and you call us primitive? Shaybons are a cross-genetic breed, sheep crossed with angora rabbits. Oh yes, you people from 2012 would not have seen those as yet. This genetic mixing was common not long after the Shameful Years, around 2070 I believe the Shaybons were bred, for use of their wool for garments to help us survive the great cold."

"Boy, I really need to put a few weeks aside so you can explain all that stuff to me," Adam said, looking at Henry, who looked as confused as he felt.

"Hang on mates," Henry laughed, "That's a joke huh? What do you get if you cross a sheep with a rabbit? A wooly jumper!" He continued laughing hysterically, yet only Adam and Trish joined in with some less intense laughter. The Denees simply looked confused.

"The machinery you say you use for engineering your weapons, how do you power it? I thought only the Denees had access to power sources?" Adam asked again.

"When did we say we have no power source? We do - though only limited use, as we can only get access to charged crystals when a defector comes to us from the Elite, and takes some crystal with him or her, if they can get to it and carry it safely. We use those crystals as we can for machinery, and to heat our shelters - but they don't last long as they have usually been well drained by the time we get them,"  Eo answered.

"Why is it so cold today?" Asked Trish, wondering whether this was anything to do with what Eo was talking about.

"Cold?" Edotha asked, "This isn't cold, it is the summer months."

"Yes I know it is, but we are usually getting temperatures anywhere from 13c to 30c at this time of year, this morning it was 3c!"

"Yes, that's what I said, it is summer." Edotha now looked puzzled.

Adam looked at Trish, then at Edotha and Eo. He thought some things through before he decided to speak.

"Could it be that when we, somehow, travelled around 350 years into the future, we have landed not only in a different civilisation, but also into a different climate?"

"Eo, you have the knowledge from your downloads, tell them what our average temperatures are year round, see if they differ much."

"Average temperatures. Winter around this area is between minus 30c and minus 3c; Spring is between minus 15c to 3c; Summer between minus 3c and 15c; Autumn is around minus 15c to 1c "Eo answered Edotha's question not much differently than if he was reading from a computer print out.

"Adam, how can this be? We are supposed to be getting warmer in the future, not colder? Those temperatures would be more than 20c colder than what we usually get, that's just crazy!" Trish looked frightened, and her voice was breaking with emotion.

"Never trusted that damn guessing with fingers crossed weather service! Ok, that's enough talk about the weather for now, lets get a plan together people, we need to get something done before every citizen in this whole damned city is murdered where they stand! Oh, sorry Trish, it's going to be ok darling, I promise you." Adam placed his arm around Trish where they sat on their couch, pulling her in close.

"It's going to be ok," he repeated, this time to try and convince himself.

# CHAPTER TWENTYNINE

It was 8.20am. Pete Green stood in his Mayoral Office at the Council Chambers and stared out of the window into what was locally called 'The Octagon'. An eight sided intersection of city streets slap bang in the middle of Duntoon city. Most of the retail outlets in the Octagon were in fact Cafes and Bars, with the odd souvenir shop thrown in for good measure. It was a beautiful city, unique in so many ways, yet most didn't appreciate it for the marvel that it was.

Mayor Green, as he was called by his staff, surveyed the empty streets outside, not one person was visible in an area that at this time of morning would usually have hundreds of people milling around, traveling one way or another, most in a hurry to get to work, or some of the more than 22,000 students trying to get to University – the top University in the Country, on time for their classes. It was a surreal sight, and one that the Mayor never thought he would see.

"Pete, have you heard some of our soldiers have been found dead at the roadblocks!" Mrs Alexandria Hastings, City Manager, abruptly barked at the Mayor. "It will be those hooligan students taking advantage of the horrendous incident that has befallen our fair city, and they need to be rounded up this minute, and I say we execute some of them to act as a warning that this will not be tolerated."

"Alexandria, we can't go around executing people, this isn't medieval times. Also, we don't know who was responsible, but it looks like it was people who have access to weapons that are very unusual in their construction. I don't believe our students would do such a terrible thing, or that they could readily get weapons like those. They may like their practical jokes, their alcohol, and some high spirited behaviour, but not killing innocent people."

"Nonsense, they found spears and bows from a crossbow. Sounds like drugged up students to me Pete! They are probably the same ones responsible for all of this, this weirdness!"

The Mayor sighed, and continued staring out of his window. He had a good heart, with good intentions, and had always put the city and its people before himself. Yet now, it seemed that something so mysterious and momentous had occurred it was beyond his ability to help put things right.

The uncomfortable silence was broken by the Mayor's phone ringing.

"Hello, Mayor Green speaking."

A Police Officer was on the other end of the phone, and spoke in a hurried voice.

"Sir, we have five people at the inner city roadblock. They are breaking the curfew, yet they say they must speak to you, as a matter of life or death."

"Well, I guess you better let them through then."

"Yes sir."

The Mayor put the phone back on its receiver, and turned to Alexandria.

"Maybe we might get some answers from these people. They say they want to talk to me about life and death issues Alexandria."

"Well then, I want to be involved in that discussion too thank you."

"Certainly, lets move to the meeting room, so we can greet them there, and hear what they have to say."

The Mayor headed out of his door, with a flustered City Manager in hot pursuit. When Adam, Trish, Henry, Edotha and Eo arrived at the Council Chambers, they were escorted to the meeting room by four soldiers, all armed with automatic weapons, and wearing balaclavas. Of course the balaclavas were accompanied by the staunch macho walk that seems compulsory to men of this type.

"Why the balaclava's fellas? Bit over the top isn't it?" Henry remarked, but he didn't get an answer.

Adam knew too well why soldiers and armed Police sometimes wore balaclavas. Firstly, to protect their identity in case at some stage in the future they need to do undercover work. Secondly, and more concerning, to hide their identity should they be required to shoot and possibly kill others, as to do so is not something one wants to be openly identified for.

Soon the five arrived at a large meeting room on the bottom floor of the building, where they saw the Mayor, the City Manager, and a secretary waiting for them. The soldiers ushered them in, with the City Manager asking two to stay guard outside the room.

"So, who are you people, and what is it that is so important you risked your life breaching the curfew?" Alexandria said to them, with it almost sounding like a demand for information rather than a question.

"Firstly, maybe introductions would be best," Trish replied, giving the City Manager a glare that most who knew Trish knew meant she was not at all impressed with bully type behaviour, nor intimidated by it. "My name is Trish Levett, this is my Husband Adam, this is Henry our friend, and this is Edotha and Eo, also friends of ours."

On hearing Trish refer to them as their friends, both Edotha and Eo smiled one of the few smiles that Trish or Adam had seen from them.

"Welcome, I am Mayor Green, and this is Alexandria our city manager."

"Mayor Green," Adam started, " we have come to you this morning to warn you of what is an imminent threat to our city, and to inform you of what we know that may shape what you do over the next few days and weeks."

"Go on," said the Mayor.

"There are two groups of people who will threaten the safety of everyone in Duntoon over the next few days, or so we believe." Adam continued, "It appears one of these groups is already present, as we have come across dead soldiers ourselves. The other group is responsible for the lights that were seen over the city last night."

"Lights? You mean the talk about UFOs?" the Mayor asked.

"Mayor Green, I know how crazy that sounds, but in comparison to what we have seen and heard in the last couple of days, believe me it is just standard fare." Adam answered.

"Can you explain what you mean by people being responsible for them, you mean it is a trick or something?" The Mayor looked at Alexandria as he spoke, who was already rolling her eyes, and sighing, obviously in an attempt to get the Mayor to stop heading down a trail that she obviously thought was all a waste of time.

"Um, yes I can, but what I am going to tell you isn't like anything you would have heard before, I know it blew me away and still does. I have to ask you to have patience in hearing me out, and to please be open minded, you are going to need to be to accept this stuff."

"I am a good listener Adam. Having the ability to listen and to have patience is what makes us human. Of course there are many who have neither attribute, and so what they can be categorised as, I am not too sure. However, I also do not bare fools lightly, and if what you tell me is part of a scam or just plain nonsense, I will tell you exactly what will happen from that moment onwards, which you may not like."

This statement from the Mayor elicited a tutting type noise from the City Manager, who also shifted in her seat, and tapped her fingers on the table in front of her. Adam decided that she obviously fell into the non-human un-categorised group. He had also decided he liked the mayor; he appeared level headed, caring and genuine. Though he may not be able to handle a crisis such as this without cracking up over the next few days, he would much rather have him in that role, supported by someone, rather than the un-categorised thing tapping her fingers.

"Mr Mayor, Edotha and Eo here are from the land at the end of the highway. I am sure you understand what I mean. They are not from Duntoon."

"Oh, you folk from Oldstown, or from down South?" Mayor Green asked.

"No, Mayor Green, I mean that are not from our time, they are from around 350 years in our future."

"For goodness sake Pete!" Alexandria shouted, "They are pulling your chain man, can't you see it! Have them locked up here and now, and lets put a stop to the mischief makers before the whole city panics!"

"We are not setting you up Mayor; I swear to you this is what we believe to be the truth from what Edotha and Eo have told us. Eo, show them your input ... thing." Adam beckoned to Eo to come forward.

At Adam's request Eo lifted his long hair, and the Mayor closely examined the silver, gently glowing spot of metal inlaid in Eo's skull.

"Oh my, what is that?" The Mayor exclaimed.

"It's a trick, that's what it is Pete!" Alexandria again interrupted.

"It is not a trick, and we are not from your future, you are from our past," Edotha answered Alexandria's claims.

"I don't know what happened to this city, but I can tell you that it has been surrounded by what can only be described as a Purple Haze, a sort of force field that no one has been able to penetrate for the last 350 years. Somehow... somehow you people, your city, vehicles, and even your climate, had been frozen in time, and only now are you seeing what has become of our World," Edotha told them all.

There was silence in the room, the Mayor looked both surprised, and sad. Alexandria continued to look indignant and arrogant, and simply tutted away as nonsense what Edotha had said.

As in everyday life, it is often those with the loudest voice or the biggest personality that overpowers meetings and force their views onto others who begrudgingly accept them, as they feel powerless at the force that appears to be within the loud-mouthed dictator before them. Meanwhile the quiet one sits, and listens, and is simply saddened as he or she hears the nonsense, knowing that in today's World loud and high-powered nonsense usually wins out over quiet common sense. Yet it was no longer 'today's World', it was the World of tomorrow, and maybe in this World the caring unassuming Mayor Pete, would rule over the loud obnoxious City Manager.

# CHAPTER THIRTY

Nicholson was an unusual man, an evil unusual man. An uncaring evil unusual man.

The term 'evil' is often banded about; often by the media or justice rights groups highlighting the horrific crimes by someone they feel is justifiably described as evil. Yet often the individual is no more evil than the average politician, but is affected by a personality disorder or mental illness, which is what controls their actions, rather than their soul, which can rightfully be the only part of humankind, referred to as evil or good. This of course brings on the question 'what is a soul'? This question may only be answered by the one who created such a thing, and maybe it is also that creator who can be the only one to make a judgment on whether that soul has become evil, for it wouldn't have started that way, would it? One belief of what a soul is, a human definition anyway, is it is the blueprint of each and every one of us, unique and detailed, and ever present. Then we must know what the definition of evil is. One definition that a Wise Man once told Adam was 'Evil - it is the non-pureness of hate and envy distilled into a force that exerts itself in a desire to cause harm and pain to all around it, which in turn motivates it to continue it's work in an ever perpetual manner through a host that has chosen to accept it, rather than it choosing it's host". Quite a mouthful and mind full, yet dissected and studied, which is what Adam did with the definition, it makes pure sense and even answers many questions.

Yet Nicholson was evil. His actions were evil, his thoughts were evil, his desires were evil, and his soul most certainly was a base for such things, and thus must be evil.

"Williams, where is your report on Area 45?"

"Nicholson ... sorry, Sir Nicholson, I am just uploading it now into the central I.T. Server."

"It takes but a second fool, why the delay? Are you as foolish and lazy as your Father was?"

"It is done Sir Nicholson." The input/output node on Williams shaved head glowed bright as it transmitted data, yet the glow faded once it had completed its task.

"Get out of my sight idiot, and report to me in exactly 24 hours to receive your orders. Get home to that mother freaking ugly Wife of yours before she gets it in her head to walk through the city and pollute it with her face." Nicholson laughed at what he believed to be an incredibly high form of humor. His three staff, other than Williams, laughed with him, more in fear at what would happen to them if they didn't rather than actually seeing any humor in his cruel remarks.

Nicholson stared ahead, as if staring into space, yet was instead seeing images of data, maps, and photos of Area 45 via the visual processing part of his brain. All this information had been collected the night before by his scouts, led by his head scout, the 'fool' Williams.

"What is this place? Central Server, search iconic history, match all photos with historic images, report immediately on finds." Nicholson barked the order, not to a person, but to the central serving computer that picked up all and any verbal commands from the inhabitants of Global City 1967. Nicholson was the leader of Global City 1967, and as such had full access to all data within the central server.

"Vehicles - match, vehicles referred to as cars, motorbike, trucks and buses, powered by fossil fuels, range from the year 1953 to 2012. Buildings - match, materials of brick, concrete, glass, steel, wood, and other natural and artificial origins. Inhabitants - match, humans approximately 109,092. Animals - match, dogs, cats, horses, cows, sheep, goats, birds, other known species, including four previously identified as extinct. Area general - match, Duntoon, New Zealand."

"So, we now know what has been hidden behind that force field, that purple cloud of arrogance that has defied our attempts to enter it all these years, Imbeciles trying to live a backward life? Or has time somehow forgotten this area 45, this area that will soon be controlled by me, this area called Duntoon,"

------------------------------------------

Eliza, Williams' wife, was not "mother freaking ugly" as described by Nicholson. Though not a beautiful woman by most people's descriptions, she was pleasant looking, and more importantly had a heart that in terms of beauty could only be described as a delicate masterpiece of art, and a mind that equaled this gift. Williams and Eliza had met on their 8th birthday, the age that all citizens of the Elite cities have their input/output node implanted.

They sat in the waiting room, feeling as nervous as anyone can who is about to have their skull drilled open, hair thin wires attached to various part of their brain, and then have a small steel plate glued in place filling the hole. They sat next to each other, yet had not met before that day and didn't speak, but occasionally exchanged anguished looks. Their Parents were waiting outside in the cafe, believing it was "good character building" to leave them by themselves waiting for the surgical prep team to take them to the pre-op room. Within ten minutes, they were holding each other's hand for comfort. They shared names with each other, and did not speak again.

"Eliza."

"Charles."

Six years later they met at a school dance, two of the junior Global Education Units had partnered up to offer the end of year dance in the force field shielded city, Eliza Sopher was a student of one unit and Charles Williams a student of the other. They literally bumped into each other as they both headed for the punch bowl, and as their eyes met, a smile formed on their faces, and on meeting again only two words were spoken. "Eliza," said Charles. "Charles," said Eliza.

The rest of the night they danced, and they fell into a World that contained only the two of them. Their smiles for each other, the touch of their hands, and the immediate love - which when true can convey more than words ever could, formed a bond that was and still is impossible to break. By the end of the night they had agreed to meet again the next day at the park, where the lack of conversation at their two previous meetings was more than made up for, sharing every detail of their life so far, their dreams and goals, and how they felt about each other. They never went more than a couple of days away from each other from that day to this day on which Eliza waited excitedly for her husband of 16 years now, to return home from his 36 hour stint at work.

"Charles," said Eliza, wrapping her arms around him, with the most wonderful smile as he entered their small apartment at the west end of Global City 1967.

"Eliza," said Charles, "I missed you so much. My scouting mission is finished now honey, and what I saw was what we have dreamed about all these years. A new life awaits us outside of this city Eliza! In a place with no force field keeping out what nature intended on sharing with us, despite how extreme it can be. A place where people go about doing the things they enjoy doing, and socialize without fearing their conversations are being monitored. A place we can truly call home. A place called Duntoon."

# CHAPTER THIRTYONE

The quintet who had met at the council chambers, where the Mayor and the city manager had been warned of the two groups who were threatening the city's security, had now retired to the council cafe.

The mayor and city manager had left Adam, Trish, Edotha, Eo and Henry to have some coffee and snacks, while they discussed what action to take next.

"Adam," Trish said, "do you think they believe us, about the time travel thing, and the Elites and Denees, and all the rest of it? I'm not sure if I still fully believe it myself."

"Well that stuck up tart Alexandria certainly didn't, but I think Mayor Green believed what we had told him, but he just couldn't really process it to accept it. You can't blame him - 350 years into the future, flying objects, force fields ... wow what a movie that would make!"

"Lucky we didn't tell him about those crystal do-wackies," Henry quipped. "That might have finished him off all together!"

"We need to find out how all of this happened, and why? Maybe we can reverse it somehow, get the World back that we once knew," Adam said.

"No, you cant, at least I don't think so." A voice came from behind where they sat, and they turned to see Kate, the Professor walking towards them.

"Kate!" Adam shouted happy to see her, "How did you get here?"

"By car. I told the soldiers who I was and if they wanted to see another few weeks alive, they better let me through to see the Mayor. I knew you guys were coming here, so I thought I better join you and let you, and the Mayor know what I think caused all of this."

"You mean, you know?" Adam asked.

"I think so, sort of at least." She hesitated, trying to think how she could present her thoughts verbally. "Its just that this sort of thing, obviously, is without precedent, so I am working purely theoretically here"

"Just one little thing," Trish said, interrupting Katie as she spoke, "Who is she Adam?"

"Oh sorry Trish, this is Kate, she's a Professor from Duntoon University. We met her when we took the Denees group there to hide them from that crazy bugger Sam. Kate, this is my Wife Trish. Kate is a Physicist, specialises in robotics, is that right Kate?"

"It is. Hello Trish, nice to meet you."

Kate shook hands with Trish, then sat down beside her.

"It looks like a little experiment two of my students were doing on alternative power sources, to power a small robot of all things, may have led to this predicament."

"Predicament!" Henry shouted, and laughed at the same time." That's one word for it sweetie, but another is catastrophe!"

"Henry. I know what has happened seems to have changed the World as we knew it, but please accept that I am a scientist and this, well, its the most amazing event that a scientist could ever dream of investigating, and so the personal aspect to it all is overshadowed for me by its scientific importance."

"It's ok Kate, go on with telling us about what you have found," Adam reassured her.

"As I said, two of my students were working on an alternative power source. They believed a certain type of crystal from Central Otago might be able to store a small charge of power, and be able to run a small machine or robot for maybe a few days before having to be replaced. However, their attempts were proving futile, so one of them decided to leave some charging cables attached to the crystals via the small robot over night. You will all remember the thunderstorm we had a few nights back? From the footage I have seen, it appears lightning struck a generator attached to the main university power supply. That charge traveled through the internal wires of our department and directly into the cables attached to the crystals. A combination of the charge from that lightning strike, the components used in the contacts of the robot, and the crystals themselves sent out a charge of its own. This charge of electricity was so great; it was like nothing anyone has ever witnessed before. In fact, it appears it was so large it had a mushroom type effect, so it didn't traumatically effect anything within the area directly inside it, but where the sides of that mushroom type charge came down, burnt anything and everything. It also looks like it literally froze, via electrical charge, everything within the mushroom - that is, within Duntoon." Kate took a deep breath, and slowly let it out. She knew what she was saying was based more on hypothesis, rather than definite data, but that was the best she had.

"What appears as only a second, or less, on the video footage, was in fact over 350 years. Immediately before the lightning strike the video time and date showed it was 12.19am 2012, within a second after the strike, it read 12.19am 2367. We didn't travel in time, we were frozen in time, only being released once the initial huge charge wore off and released the mushroom effect."

"My Mum, I wont see her again will I?" Trish suddenly said, and began to cry.

Adam comforted Trish, putting his arm around her and offering her hope.

"Sweetie, you don't know that for sure. Who knows what might happen in the coming months, maybe she is out there somewhere, somehow. You have to keep her in your heart and in your thoughts, because as long as you do that, she is with you always."

Henry briefly spoke, in a hushed tone. "Hope, the one thing so simple to have, yet so powerful in getting you through any and every situation. Lose hope, lose everything." He smiled gently at Trish, and placed a hand on her shoulder.

"So Kate. You mean this, explosion for want of a better term; it acted like a sort of bubble? Trapping all of Duntoon inside it, and somehow freezing it for what appeared to be a second, but was over 350 years?" Adam asked.

"I believe so Adam."

"But what about the camera that you say recorded the lightning strike hitting the crystals in the robot, why did it show a jump in time, when we didn't notice anything. I mean, how would it know?"

"A good question Adam. I have asked myself the same thing, and haven't come up with an answer - yet. Though I think it has something to do with the actual electrical charge that was emitted by the crystals when they were hit. You know how a magnet can sometimes affect a watch, the charge from the magnet in some cases can literally speed up the mechanism, or slow it down, changing the time by maybe a few seconds or even a few minutes, in just a second or two. It is possible the charge acted on the timing of the camera, somehow speeding it up, incredibly, within less than a second. But then, maybe there is another answer, it's way to early to say, it could take years to work out exactly what happened."

There was a commotion outside the cafe, and on turning towards it the group saw several soldiers run past, towards the main entrance shouting. Then, they heard gunfire, several shots, then screams and shouting again.

"Henry, Eo, you guys come with me. Trish, Edotha, Kate - stay here, and lock the door if you can, barricade it even," Adam shouted as he headed towards the exit.

"Adam!" Trish shouted back at him, "Stay here, don't leave us."

"No, we need to see what's happening. It'll be ok, I promise."

Henry and Eo joined Adam as he headed out the door of the cafe, and along the corridor towards the main council entrance. When they were just a few metres from the entrance they could clearly see 40 to 50 Denees, gathered there, there were four bodies, all Denees, on the ground bleeding. All the soldiers though had been overpowered, and had had their weapons taken from them. One soldier had an arrow from a crossbow embedded in his left shoulder, a companion sat with him, doing his best to stop the bleeding and keep him calm.

"You two stay in here; let me go talk with them," Eo said to Adam and Henry.

"You sure you will be safe?" Adam asked him, concerned.

"Yes, I know the leader, leave it to me."

Eo walked outside. At first the others didn't seem to realise he was also a Denee, and three of them rushed at him, until they were stopped in their tracks by a command coming from behind them.

"Leave him!" A stocky middle aged Denee shouted at them. "He is one of us."

"One of you I am not," Eo replied. "I am not a murdering piece of scum like you Northern lot. Rauner, I thought you were dead."

"Oh Eo, my friend, nothing and no one can kill me, I am way too smart, only fools like you die at a young age."

"You are not smart, you are a Sociopathic fool, who even death rejects, which is the only reason you still breathe."

"What kind of welcome is that, to your new leader Eo? Look at this place; it's full of food, shelter, vehicles - primitive, but vehicles all the same. Now, it is mine, all of it, and my people will use it to live an easier life, and to help us overpower those Elite filth."

"You are no leader Rauner, you are a nobody. Where is your Eo, let me talk with him."

"Oh him." Rauner laughed. "He disobeyed me when I ordered him to kill the family we came across as we entered this once protected area. So, I killed him, then I personally killed the family." He smirked, as if proud of his achievement.

Rauner was, like so many so-called leaders, so in love with himself and so over sure of his own abilities that reality and the preciousness of life meant little to nothing to him.

"Enter the building, take everyone in there hostage, and kill anyone who resists," Rauner ordered his group. "Eo, you, my foolish Elite Outcast, will show us where Princess Amberley is. I know she never travels without you nearby."

--------------------------------------------------

The Elite soon rounded up all who were inside the council chambers, including the Mayor and a very annoyed and indignant City Manager. However, there were a certain five people who were missing, whose names were Adam, Henry, Trish, Edotha and a pretty Professor called Kate.

Adam and Henry had watched and listened to the exchange between Eo and the maniac who went by the name Rauner, and had quickly moved to warn Trish and the other two. They had then left the now unguarded back entrance of the council chambers, and fled to a nearby street, that via another route would lead them to the University campus.

As they moved quickly along the street towards where their companions were still housed up at the University, Adam questioned Edotha.

"That man, Rauner, is he from the Northern Denees? Is he their leader or what?"

"Leader?" Edotha laughed, though in a belittling way, "You have to be kidding me. He's the Dictator of the Northern Denee's that's for sure, but he certainly does not qualify for the title of leader. When you understand how the World changed over the 350 years that you missed out on, you will see that some who became Denees, did so more by default than by design. Rauner is from a long line of criminals, murderers, and anti-social misfits who gained a following by using fear, not courage."

"But there must have been 50 followers with him, why do they follow a mad man for, with such blind obedience?"

"It is our way. Once a person earns a place as one to be followed, or in Rauner's case, forced his way into the position, it is all for one, and one for all."

Henry chuckled as he listened in to what Edotha had to say. "I see some of them old sayings just keep going, no matter how many years pass."

"I saw the same thing when we came across your group, how they all put their weapons down, and followed you when you surrendered to us, no resistance," Adam said.

"Yes, as I said, it is our way. We are a people who have been taken advantage of for so many years, centuries, we will fight when we believe we can win, or when we see that we must do so for the survival of our group. But when one of us falls, and we can see that others will also fall with no good coming from the losses, we will surrender to the more powerful force."

"It's a complex culture you have, not simplistic at all - which is how you first appeared to me. I am sorry for judging you so quickly. One thing I am totally puzzled by though, is what is so important about this Princess Amberley? Rauner seems very interested in finding her, and why is she called Princess?"

"There are only four in the royal group, around the entire World. Princess Amberley is one of those four."

"Royal group? What makes them the royal group?" Adam asked Edotha, getting impatient of the somewhat cryptic answers she was giving him, yet again.

"Only those in the royal group, Adam, know where the key is kept, and where the area is that can only be accessed by the use of that key."

"Yeah, well that doesn't really explain anything." Adam said, with a definite edge to his voice this time "What area, what key, what the heck are you going on about Edotha? I'm sorry, but this weirdness, well, it is just starting to get just too much, you know?"

"Over 350 years have passed between your time, and ours. What do you expect, everything should be the same? The key will unlock a door, or at least I believe it is a door of some sort, that will lead into an area that will explain a secret of such significance - well, human's will never be the same again once they understand it, as it is all empowering. It is this reason that it is guarded by limiting those who know where the key and the doorway are, to only four people at any one time. Those four are known as the royal group, and the Elite, along with Rauner and a few other crazies, will do anything they can to get to one of the royal four, and to the key. The royal four, also have hypersensitive senses, and can detect many things that others are not able to. This makes them very valuable to others, especially to leaders and mad men like Rauner."

They reached the University building where Princess Amberley, apparently one of the royal four that Edotha spoke of, hid along with Thomas, Larry, Richie and the other Denees that Edotha and Eo left behind.

# CHAPTER THIRTYTWO

Charles Williams did not like Nicholson - the leader of Global City 1967.

Williams had met Nicholson while still at the Global Education unit, which all the Elite attended within their designated city of residence, from the age of eight years to the age of nineteen. Many of those years were indoctrinating them into the beliefs that all Elite must accept and the rules of which they must follow. The output/input node is implanted into their skull, and attached to several parts of their brain at age eight before they start their education. This 'node' allows the central server to upload facts that they need to know at various ages as they progress through the Elite's education system.

Charles was 16 when he met Nicholson, who was one of a rare few transferred from another Global City due to his Father being an Information Technology expert whose skills were needed due to some faults with the central server.

Nicholson was a man of high intelligence, whose uploads from the central server of his previous city, and city 1967, contained far more data than the average citizen. This was due to his Father's position, and his determination to be above and beyond that of any ordinary man or woman. Nicholson used Charles from the day he met him, pretending to befriend him, but really taking him on more as a personal servant than a true friend.

"Eliza, I have received an message via the server from Nicholson," Charles called out to his Wife, who was busy preparing a delicious meal for the man she loved so dearly. They shared meal preparation, as they both loved to be able to do something special for their partner. A culinary delight is but one of many ways to show one's love for another.

"Oh, from that dreadful man. What does it say?" Eliza asked, dreading her husband's answer.

"He is planning on sending in an invasion force tomorrow night at 10pm. 2500 troops, with me leading a scout force of 20 an hour before the attack to mark landing zones."

"Oh Charles, I thought you said this Duntoon place would be a new home for us, where we could escape Nicholson and the ways of this city?"

"It can be Eliza, it can be. We will need to leave soon though, and prepare the inhabitants of Duntoon for fighting back against Nicholson and his men. Without us, they don't stand a chance."

-------------------------------------------------

After the escapees of the council chambers ambush and those who were hiding out at the University exchanged greetings, Adam and Trish met with Edotha and Princess Amberley in a small room away from where the others now rested.

"So - I guess the question is, what now?" Adam said to the three who looked at him hoping he had answers rather than questions.

"We need to reunite back with the rest of our people, I think that's the only way we can then help you fight off the northern Denees, and the worse that is yet to come." Edotha replied.

"Princess Amberley, you haven't spoken. What do you think of all this?" Trish asked the petite young woman who sat at the table, looking very calm, yet a little bewildered.

"I have nothing to say. Why speak if the words you have are only excess noise, rather than words of wisdom or relief."

"Great, another one who speaks in riddles," Adam mumbled, more to himself than for sharing with his companions.

"Adam, Princess Amberley is one of only four in the World who are as special as a person can be. She, like the other three Royals, only speaks when she has something to share that is of great importance, or brings relief to the hearts and minds of those around her," Edotha explained.

Adam thought about what Edotha had said, and realised that this gift, rule, custom, or whatever it was, was maybe the way everyone should be with their words. To only speak when it brings comfort to others, or shares wisdom, could surely only result in a World that was a better place for all rather than the World that had maybe come to an end a few days ago for Adam and the others in Duntoon. Adam thought back to when he was listening to the Mayor speak, and the City Managers interjections, and how he then wondered whether this new World would bring about a change to who held the power. Those who spoke with thought and care, or those who spoke with volume and malice? It appeared that the 'Royal Four' of the Denees, were certainly laying a path for what should be a journey that everyone attempts to travel.

Trish stared at Adam intensely before she spoke. "Adam, shouldn't we warn the rest of Duntoon about these people who are invading our city. Surely with the tens of thousands who live here, we can as a group defeat 50 or so Denees!"

"Fifty?" Edotha asked. "You think there are only 50? Trish, these are just a small group who are investigating what is in this area. Remember it has been sealed in the purple haze for over 350 years. There will be maybe another 5000 to 10,000 on their way, as soon as the scouts get back to them and advise them of what they have found."

"Well, sounds like somehow, we need to ensure the scouts don't get back to the others," Adam said to Edotha.

Princess Amberley stood, and looked into the faces of the other three, one by one.

"Elite are coming, only a few minutes away. I can sense them, we need to be prepared."

After Princess Amberley had spoken, she left the room, immediately followed by Edotha, and a puzzled Adam and Trish, tightly holding each other's hand.

The Princess led the three followers into the large room where the other Denees, as well as Thomas, Henry, Kate, Larry and Richie waited. Larry and Richie were staring out one of the narrow windows that had an outside view. As the Princess and the others entered the room, Larry turned to them.

"Dudes, you better take a look at this. Bro, it's frigging awesome."

Adam, along with Kate who had been ignoring her two students until now, rushed to the window. There they saw a light in the sky, it seemed to hover in the same place, not far from the building they were in, but too high to see any real detail. It wasn't like a star, or the stereotypical 'UFO' with flashing lights and a giant spinning saucer like shape. Instead it gave out a fairly gentle glow, a little like a pearl coloured low watt light bulb would do in a dimly lighted room.

Princess Amberley joined them at the window.

"It's them, the Elite - I could feel the vibrations from their craft. Hide, its the only chance you have of surviving, and ambush them if you can - as that will be the only opportunity to destroy them, before they destroy you," she said to those who were staring at the craft, and to the rest of the people in the large meeting room.

The Denees left the room almost the second the Princess had finished speaking.

Richie laughed, "Ha, man they are like little robots, and you are like their programmer huh? Choice." He high fived Larry, who looked a little surprised at how Richie seemed to be treating it all like a demonstration in one of their robotics lectures.

"Where are they going?" Trish asked.

Edotha, who had also started making her way to the exit of the room, stopped, turned and answered her. "They are going to hide, did you not hear Princess Amberley? Get out of here now, if you want to live past tonight."

With some hesitation and worried glances at each other, they all eventually headed for the exit, except the Princess.

"What about you then, why aren't you going to hide?" Trish asked the Princess, who was still standing by the window, looking at the craft that was now slowly descending.

"Because they will not harm me, I am their prize treasure. I will be a good distraction, giving you the opportunity to plan an ambush before they leave the building with me in their custody."

Adam grabbed Trish's hand, pulling her towards the exit.

"Come on; let's just do as she says huh? We will worry about the details later!" He told her.

Within a few minutes the entire group had hidden in various offices, cupboards and other rooms around the building. Adam and Trish had selected an office, where they hid behind a large desk, only to be surprised and a little annoyed that Richie and Larry were also hiding in the same place.

"Dudes!" Larry said, smiling.

Princess Amberley remained in the large meeting room, still watching the craft. It was now only two metres from the ground, and around 30 metres from the building. As it touched down, its shape and detail could be clearly seen.

This Elite craft was only small, accommodating up to a maximum of four people. It was powered by what was called an 'eighth crystal', being an Otago Mountain Crystal an eighth of an inch square in size. The craft was white on the outside, very similar to a semi gloss heavy duty plastic. With one large window at the front, it was around 6 metres in length, and 3 metres in width, and just over 2 metres high, yet had no corners as such as it was all one smooth almost egg shaped craft.

Princess Amberley finally moved away from the window, and strolled slowly to a chair and sat down, placing her arms on the table in front of her, looking calm and serene.

-------------------------------------------------

They had now been waiting for at least fifteen minutes, tucked in behind the large desk, which was no doubt the desk of a professor at the University. Larry and Richie were leaning against the legs of the desk, eyes closed, "chilling" according to Richie. Where as Adam and Trish sat hard against each other, still holding hands, anxious and tense, but at peace with the World because they had each other.

Hand holding is rarely seen these days, Trish thought to herself. It appears to be smirked at, as though it is a sign of weakness, a sign of insecurity and inferiority. Many of the very financially rich couples seem to rarely hold hands, they instead let their designer clothes, bags, shoes and hairstyles speak to others about how they view the World, and each other. Those in love, or having a deep love or caring for the other, hold hands and no thought goes into what others think or feel about them. Perhaps that is why divorces in the twenty-first century have reached an all time high, because of something as simple as a lack of hand holding and more significantly the sentiment and meaning behind it.

Adam and Trish were happy to hold hands in any situation, in fact to them - there was little else in life they would rather do when they were together, at least in public. The feel of the other's hand gave them energy, sustenance, and warmed their heart, no matter how cold this new World was and no matter what new danger approached them - they were at peace.

Soon there was the sound of footsteps in the corridor outside the office where the four in hiding were stationed. The footsteps stopped momentarily, and Trish felt her heart skip a beat - or two. The footsteps soon started again though, getting quieter as they moved further down towards the meeting room where Princess Amberley apparently waited for them, using herself as bait in the hope it may offer her companions the chance of survival.

Adam tapped Richie on the arm, as he sat there still with his eyes closed, and half a smile on his face.

"We need to move, see if we can come in behind these Elites, or whoever the heck they are. Hang on, um, you guys are stoned aren't you?"

"Ha, yeah, a bit. Man, we needed something to relax our nerves Dude. It's been an intense day you know."

"Oh no, typical bloody students," Trish mumbled.

Adam couldn't help but smile, even though he was fuming with anger at their stupidity.

"Well, stoned or not, Richie, Larry - you two come with me. Trish, sweetheart, stay here, hide under the desk, please. I'll come back for you once we deal with these guys."

"No way Adam! You are not leaving me here, I will come, and fight too - if I have to."

Adam could see the determination in Trish's eyes, and knew there was no point in arguing with her. He kissed her on the forehead. "Darling, you have as much right as I do to confront these people, and see what we can do but just be careful, please. Ok, lets go."

As they approached the meeting room, Adam immediately saw a scene he certainly didn't expect. Rather than heavily armed futuristic soldiers, he saw a middle aged couple, who were sitting at the table with the Princess, talking calmly with her, even smiling at her. She didn't appear the least bit frightened or threatened.

The four walked into the room, feeling it was safe, yet as they did, the man smiled, stood and faced them, and raised a hand sized silver coloured object, pointing it directly at them.

"Greetings Duntoon inhabitants, please stay where you are or I will destroy you within seconds."

Larry walked towards the man, ignoring his warning.

"Dude, just chill, we just want to know what you want man, nothing else."

There was a flash of light and a high pitched sound, both lasting no more than a fraction of a second. Larry dropped to the ground instantaneously. Richie ran to him, where he lay motionless on the floor of the meeting room.

"Larry, man, you ok? What the hell did you do to him freak!"

"He's ok, but one more attempt to move towards my Wife or me, before I say its ok to do so, and I will change the setting from stun to destroy. The energy burst has merely interrupted the circuits of his brain, rendering instant unconsciousness, he will wake in about 10 to 12 minutes."

He smiled, as if he had just explained the workings of a kitchen blender he was selling, then continued his mini speech.

"My name is Charles, Charles Williams. This is my beautiful and wonderful Wife, Eliza."

Eliza smiled, but chose not to speak. Trish immediately smiled back at her, though she didn't intend on doing so after seeing Larry hit the ground, but somehow she felt that Eliza, and hopefully Charles, were good people. There was something about them she couldn't quite put her finger on, but it seemed non-threatening and almost reassuring, which made no sense at all in the circumstances.

"I am the head scout for Global City 1967. In a short time, unless we act, a man by the name of Nicholson will send many soldiers into Area 45, which of course you know as Duntoon, and will no doubt destroy almost all of its inhabitants, unless he believes there is a useful purpose to keep them alive."

Eliza then suddenly spoke, as if she wanted to quickly right any wrongful judgment of her Husband's actions.

"Charles is not a violent man, despite what you have just seen. Both he and I want to help you, and you in return help us have a new life here, in your city. Charles, tell them what can be done."

Adam interrupted before Charles had a chance to speak again.

"So I take it you guys are the Elite? What is it with people in the future and their desire to kill people? If it's not the Denees, it's the Elite. I thought our society was a violent rotten one, but from the looks of things, it has deteriorated even more over the years."

Charles lowered his weapon and placed it in a holster at his side. He then invited them to come and sit at the table. Once they were sitting, he helped Richie carry Larry to a large table, and lay him on it where they could see him, and check he recovered without any problems with his airway.

Adam, Trish and Richie introduced themselves, though with bitterness in their voices. They were not sure whether they could trust this man.

"Do you know what created the force-field that has kept us out for so many years, and frozen you in time - or at least that is what I am guessing has happened?" Charles asked the group.

"Richie, explain to Charles the theory that Professor Kate and you two came up with," Adam prompted.

Richie explained the best he could about the robot, the crystals, the lightning strike, the purple flash and so on. Charles listened intently, every now and then making sounds such as "Argh", and "Oh", and comments such as "What, ha-ha, I see". He continually glanced at his wife, and though Eliza made similar remarks, they were made quietly, and more to herself than the group as a whole.

"So, does that make any sense to you, Charles?" Adam asked.

"Well, yes and no. But the main thing is, I think Eliza, my darling Wife, understands it completely and may be able to recreate the force-field around this city, one that doesn't freeze time, but only physical in nature that will keep Nicholson and his military out of here. Is that right dear? You can do that? I am sure you can, you are amazing." Charles smiled at Eliza, who smiled back at him.

"I believe so my husband, I believe so. I will need the crystals you used, and some of the alloy that connected them to your robot - Mama 01?" She let out a short, but polite laugh.

"Dude?" Richie asked towards Adam. "You think that's ok?"

Adam looked at Princess Amberley. She nodded her head.

"Well I guess if royalty is approving of it, then we should go for it."

# CHAPTER THIRTYTHREE

Larry started to come to, with a few moans and groans, maybe more for dramatic effect than any real need, and he slowly sat up.

"Man, what happened?"

"Just a wee shock my friend. You have to understand, I love my Wife more than anyone could ever imagine, and I had to stop you as I didn't know whether you meant her harm or not. It appears you are peaceful. I apologise, but it will have no lasting effects," Charles reassured Larry, and walked over to him, placing his hand on his shoulder.

"Wow, that was awesome dude! I have to get one of those things!"

Everyone but Princess Amberley laughed at Larry's remarks, which helped ease the tension some more.

Eliza stood, "You, Richie? Take me to where you have the crystals, and where the rest of your 'Mama' is, so I can see about getting this city of yours protected. If we don't hurry, Nicholson will get here, then we are all as good as dead, or worse still," Her voice faded as she spoke the last few words.

"Worse still?" Trish asked. "What could be worse than dead?"

"Death brings an end and many believe a new beginning. Being enslaved by Nicholson, brings relentless pain and mockery, where every bit of your pride is attacked on almost a daily basis," Eliza answered.

"Slavery? What the hell? I thought you guys are in our future, Earth's future, how can there be slavery in 2367?" Adam was fuming, and it showed in the tone and volume of his voice.

"There is so much you need to be filled in on Adam, but Eliza needs to get to work now, or you will experience first hand what it is that she talks of."

As a group they agreed that Richie, and Larry now that he was recovered from his "wee shock" would accompany Eliza to where they had hidden the lead trap that still contained the crystals. They would then take her to the University's robotics building where the pieces of their robot, Mama-001, still remained. Charles however, insisted she take his weapon, just in case they came across any undesirables, though it was obvious he still did not totally trust the two young men or the others.

Only minutes after the three left the room, Edotha entered. "Princess, are you ok?"

"Yes Edotha, these Elite do not mean any harm. I believe they too are trying to escape what we have fought off all of our lives."

"She's right," said Charles. "We have been living in the Global City, it is true. My Wife and I have had full access, well, almost full access, to the central server and have had almost all the downloads that are possible. Yet we hated the culture of a select few telling us what we should believe, what we should do, and how we should do it. We have dreamed of the shielded area for many years, we always believed it would be our escape, our freedom."

"How do we know we can trust you? You Elite have hunted us for the last two hundred years, using us as slaves, taking the food we so needed, and searching for crystal like hungry wolves."

"We did as Nicholson ordered us to, as we had no other choice. If you don't obey, you face consequences, including death if that was what he decided was fitting."

"Ok, you two. Looks like we need to just focus on the now, and forget the past. Which isn't easy for me to say, as our whole World is now the past! But you work with what you have, you know what I mean? Charles, can you explain to us how on earth all of this came about? I mean, you Elite, the Denees, why it's so frigging cold!" Adam asked, not just as a distraction to hopefully put an end to the accusations and tension, but also to get the answers he, Trish and no doubt everyone in Duntoon so needed.

"Very well, I will try and give you a basic idea of some of what you have not been a party to. From 2012 through to now, so much has happened, particularly in the 88 years from 2012 to 2100." Charles paused, looked at his hands, as if they were covered in notes for the speech he was about to give, but after turning them from front to back, and back to front, he realised neither his hands nor anyone in the room could help him with what he was about to divulge.

"I guess, stupidity, greed, ignorance and the remarkable power of the News Media in your day is what led to what exists now. A few select people, Adam, led the World's Governments, and much of the population along a road that was the exact opposite of where they should have been heading."

"Ok, stop there for a moment Charles. Sorry, but if you are going to talk in metaphors and speak in riddles like Edotha often does, this really isn't going to be helpful for my or Trish's understanding. So, please, just keep to the facts, ok?" Adam asked of Charles.

"Certainly. The environment Adam, it was Earth's environment that led people to do things, and believe things, that in turn led to many hundreds of thousands dying. Firstly from starvation, crime, and disease, and then they were killed."

"So, this damn Global Warming thing huh? It really starts killing us all off? Man, I thought it was a load of crap personally," Adam quipped.

Charles looked at him, with a puzzled look, then began to laugh, more and more, louder and louder, until tears rolled down his face as he became near hysterical.

"Hey, hey. Calm down Charles, I can't see what is so funny about people dying! I take it you are laughing at my ignorance, about not realising what an impact the Global Warming was to have."

"Oh no," Charles, almost choked as he spoke and laughed at the same time, "quite the opposite my friend, quite the opposite!"

"Yet again, this is all just very confusing. We asked for answers Charles, not to be mocked," Trish said crossly, which had the effect of stopping Charles's laughing almost instantly.

Charles wiped the tears from his face. "I apologise Trish, Adam. But, when you understand, you will see why I laughed. Oh boy. Ok, Global Warming was a complete and utter nonsense, yet despite the World getting colder and colder, as it actually started to do even before the year you came from, in fact official unaltered records showed it started cooling in 2001, this didn't stop the giant business machine from working. By 2035, taxes had been increased to amounts you couldn't begin to imagine. They had to be, to pay the carbon credits now demanded by the Billionaire owned companies and now Billionaire forest owners. Many hundreds of thousands in New Zealand, and millions around the World were made homeless. Only the very rich could now afford to have homes, and vehicles. Petrol almost quadrupled in price year after year, until in 2035 petrol in this country was at $48 per litre!"

"You are freaking kidding me, $48 a litre! I thought it was bad enough in 2012 at $2.35 a litre!"

"Oh yes, and it went higher than that, until in 2040 when the power of the Otago Mountain Crystal was discovered, and suddenly an alternative power source was found. Yet by then, the World was entering the giant freeze, a new ice age."

"An ICE AGE!" Trish shouted, "Sorry, I mean, an ice age? How could that be, we are supposed to be getting warmer?"

"As I said Trish, the World began cooling in 2001, though at that stage the cooling per year was only minute. This did not stop the Global Warming Business drivers though. They simply changed the name to, what was it, oh yes, 'Climate Change'". Charles laughed again. "Now, it seems ridiculous how any person with any sense at all could buy that. How they could simply change the science to suit the facts, yet still claim that the cooling was caused by warming, which was caused by man, which meant you all needed to pay more taxes!" Charles stared at Adam intently.

"What? Why are you staring at me?" Adam asked, a little nervous about this man from the future, and his unusual story of the past, yet Adam and Trish's future, which they had missed. It was all very confusing to Adam.

"I am wondering whether those in the early 2000's were maybe a little, well, let me think of a description, slow? How could anyone believe the scam that was perpetrated on to you all, and obviously all in the name of money, yet claiming it was to save your lives? With the end result of course, it killed so many of you instead." Charles paused, looking at Trish and Adam with pity.

"You see Adam, Trish, as the World cooled, the need for heat obviously increased tenfold, yet with the huge increases in electricity, the ban on burning fossil fuels, people literally froze to death, unable to afford the heating supplies."

"So, it was all a con after all! This whole damn emission-trading scheme that was forced on so many of us, a con, a scam!" Adam raised his voice, and he stood and paced around the room, punching his hand.

"Oh I believe originally it was all well intended. A few scientists, well, more like weather forecasters really, seeking some fame, thought they had discovered something, a warming of the Earth that was being caused by little old humankind. Funny enough, the same weather forecasters had only a short while before this claim, claimed we were entering an ice age, yet the media and public ignored that, but when they mentioned warming, and it was being caused by mankind, every man and his dog who thought 'here is an easy way to make a buck', were suddenly very interested! An ex-politician, a few movie stars, and oh yes off it went like a forest fire! People took notice, they believed the nonsense, which was what it was to any serious scientist of course, and they sought an answer to the dreaded warming of the Earth that was going to 'destroy mankind'! We humans are interesting creatures, it's almost like we thrive on pending disaster. If it wasn't tales of asteroids hitting the earth, it was the sun burning out, or a black hole being generated by a man made machine or by mankind causing the Earth to warm and killing us all. One thing none of us interested in history can understand is how you all accepted that $CO_2$ was a bad thing, and you had to somehow put a stop to it? $CO_2$ is the lifeblood of the planet, our plants and trees survive on it, animals survive on them, and us humans survive from reliance on both plants and animals. Also, that doesn't even factor in that the vast majority of $CO_2$ production was out of your hands, in fact I believe something like 97% or 98% comes from volcanoes, bacteria, animals and alike, and only a tiny fraction of it was coming from your antiquated machinery and transportation vehicles" Charles smiled, not from amusement this time, but more so as a full-stop to what he was saying, as his Wife Eliza, along with Richie and Larry reentered the room, pulling the trolley with the trap, along with some robotic bits and pieces sitting on top of it.

# CHAPTER THIRTYFOUR

At the Council Chambers Eo was standing up to Rauner, the maniacal leader of the Northern Denees who had taken the mayor, city manager, Eo and around a dozen others hostage.

"I won't take you to the Princess, so give it up Rauner. You do not deserve to even lay your eyes on her, let alone to converse with her," Eo told Rauner, without emotion, yet as staunch as any man can be.

"Then, you shall die Eo, right here, and right now."

"Then you will have no Eo, and no chance of gaining any more stolen downloads from the Elite's cities."

"Hm. You may have a point Eo, considering I killed our useless Elite Outcast, I sort of need you - or do I? Ok, you will live, but I'm still pissed off, so someone else shall die."

No sooner had Rauner finished speaking, when he suddenly turned to a Council administrator, and stabbed him in the chest, again and again. The man fell, his mouth open, uttering a single word as he hit the ground, "Why?"

Rauner laughed, and kicked him in the side of his now blood soaked body where he lay on the ground.

"These Duntoonians, they die like cowards, like the first two on the farm with the horses and all those damn stupid though very tasty goats." He laughed again, then turned his attention to the twenty or so other Denees who were in the same meeting room with him, Eo and some other hostages.

"I want ten scouts to volunteer to head back to our land, and guide our fighters here."

Within just a few seconds, ten of his people had come forward and volunteered to head back to where the many thousand other Northern Denees waited, and wondered.

"Go, go now! Bring our people here; I want 2000 of our soldiers here within two days. I want them to bring all their weapons. Then instruct the rest of our people to follow them in seven days time, when we will have secured this city as ours, and we will use it as our new base. Any Duntoon residents who stand in our way are to be cut down like the pathetic backward thinking dogs that they are."

-------------------------------------------------

The group watched Eliza working with the two now very excited students, Larry and Richie. Within just two hours Eliza had drawn up plans of how she was going to manipulate parts of the now many-pieced robot, along with one of the crystals, into a force field generating device that would protect the whole of Duntoon.

"But Eliza, surely when it took a lightning strike and all four crystals to originally form the force field that froze us in time for over 350 years, it will take more than just one crystal to now form a force field around the city?" Adam asked.

"I believe Adam the fact that you had the power of the whole four crystals, along with the power from the lightning strike, and the metal alloy the boys used on the contacts was simply too much power. It was of such force that it literally interfered with what I call the hyaloplasm of time itself. We do not want to do the same again, or goodness knows where we will end up, time wise. Instead, I want to generate an electrical field that will arc around and over this area, that does not interfere with time, yet will stop anyone and anything passing through it," Eliza replied, with the gentle, caring, yet knowledgeable smile they had all seen earlier still on her face as she spoke.

When she had finished speaking, she spoke to Larry and Richie about other equipment they would need. Richie hurried from the room to get the other items, while Larry and Eliza set up a make shift lab in the back corner of the room.

"My Wife is a genius my friends. Watching her work is like watching an artist create a work of art, yet what she produces far outweighs the marvels of art and instead enters the realms of creation itself." Charles smiled with pride as he spoke, and the love for his Wife was evident in everything he did. The way he spoke, his body language, the light in his eyes, all shed warmth that was for one person and one person only, his Wife Eliza.

"Charles, can I ask you something?" Trish said. "Can I ask you what the term Denees and the term Elite actually refer to? It has been bothering me since I first heard the words used."

"The answer is quite complex in some ways, yet in others very simple. I will do my best to explain Trish. With the whole climate change scam, two groups became evident, and bigger and stronger as the years went past. Those who tried to expose the hoax for what it was were called Deniers. They were compared to deniers of the World War Two Holocaust, to deniers of evolution; even to denying the World was round. This was done purposely by the hugely powerful business machine that drove the hoax. They purposely tried to shame people from admitting they thought it was a hoax, to prevent people from speaking out as they would be afraid of ridicule and anger from others. In fact if you know the ancient story called 'The Emperors New Clothes' it was exactly the same basic principal. Some con artists shaming people into saying what they wanted to be said, even though deep down those same people knew it was a nonsense."

"Yes, you are right Charles, even leading up to 2012 this was starting to happen," Adam agreed.

"Oh it became a lot worse from around 2014 onwards Adam. The scammers started demanding laws be introduced banning anyone, and I mean anyone and everyone, from speaking out against the climate change promoters. They demanded jail terms, and by 2016 many Countries introduced the draconian laws to appease the business giants, who were now raking in hundreds of billions of dollars in carbon credits. By 2023, jail terms were not enough, as the cold temperatures were starting to make even the most avid Greenie start to question the so-called science. So, the climate change con men and con women demanded death penalties be introduced to anyone who publicly questioned their 'science'. Within two years, some countries agreed to that request, and people started to be executed. By 2027 even New Zealand had introduced the death penalty for one and only one crime, the crime now termed 'Climate Change Denial'."

"That's ludicrous! Sounds like a crazy sci fi story rather than reality!" Adam stated, with anger in his voice.

"It is also crazy and idiotic to believe that humans and cows can change a Planet's climate, when for millions of years other more populous amounts of creatures had inhabited the planet and had no effect on the climate. When CO2 levels had been tens of times higher in the past, and there was no evidence they had caused the Earth to warm. Yet Adam, that is what many people, even in your year believed. Yet, there was no actual proof. There wasn't even any reliable evidence backing the claims, but because the climate change propagandists told people this was so, and the media loved hearing every word of the apocalyptic claims because it sold their papers and achieved higher views, people just accepted what they were told. Sure, the promoters of the scam continually fed out temperature figures showing what they liked to call a 'warming trend', yet they didn't make it well known that they only took temperatures from weather stations that showed a warming trend, and ignored the many that showed cooling trends, nor that they continually 'adjusted' the temperature recordings. They then started claiming the ocean levels were rising due to huge ice melts – but reliable records showed the ocean level increases were nothing different from natural variations that have occurred for millions of years. Eventually the deniers, had to go underground, out of the sight and hearing of the media and climate change supporters. They became the 'Denees'. Where as the now Billionaire Climate Change scam artists, and their somewhat brainwashed followers, became elitist, and so they became known as the 'Elite'."

Adam continued to pace back and forth, shaking his head, and mumbling to himself about "Climate change scam artists!", "Global warming - global damn freezing, the fools!" "Gore - I knew he was a …" He mumbled the last few words, deciding that others in the room may not appreciate the type of description he had reserved for Mr Gore. "If only people had really thought about that nonsense they were feeding us, if only they had followed where the money was going. Damn it all!

Charles looked over at Trish, who had nearly fallen asleep. It was 2.30am, and the day had taken its toll physically, emotionally and mentally on them all.

"You should find somewhere comfortable to have a lie down Trish. Why don't you go home and sleep there, take Adam with you. Eliza and the boys will keep working on the crystals, and I have no doubt they will get your city protected from Nicholson, and those Denees who wish you harm," Charles told her, in what could only be described as a Fatherly tone of voice.

"How could we do that Charles? There are murderers out there, and not just the Denees, but the soldiers will no doubt shoot anything that moves because of the curfew and the killings. Besides, it feels like a family here, these people, the Princess, Richie, Larry, Henry and the others, they all seem like my family now. Now that my Mother, is, is …" She couldn't quite get the words out, yet she didn't cry.

Trish felt angry now, angry at what had happened with the crystals locking them in time, and locking her Mother out. Angry at how over 350 years of the development of mankind, or should that be the all but self-destruction of mankind, has passed by in an instant of a second to her and all the other inhabitants of Duntoon. Also angry at how they, the people of her time, had been so foolish letting the very rich make themselves richer, no doubt laughing at the rest of mankind as they used the excuse of "saving the planet" to in fact bring mankind to its knees.

The hours ticked by, and the other Denees along with Kate and Henry who had been hiding slowly joined the group, listened to Charles's story and shook hands with him under the approval and encouragement of the Princess. The room had grown silent, as some of the group slept, and others had fallen into almost a trance like state, half from tiredness and half from the intrigue of watching Eliza with the help of the two students, transform a few dozen electrical components and one of the crystals into what looked like a digital clock with a jumper lead attached to it, with an elaborate large open fuse at the other end. The crystal sat in the middle of the device safely resting on a small bed of lead pieces with a sprinkling of ground-up alloy.

Eliza took a step back from the device, smiled at Richie, then at Larry, and announced, "It is done my friends, now just to switch it on."

Everyone crowded around to watch, with Kate naturally taking a special interest, and as Eliza bent to slide what appeared to be a simple slide type switch to the on position, a loud voice spoke out, coming from behind the gathering.

"So, here you all are. What the hell do you weirdoes think you are doing?"

It was Sam, he had returned, and he was armed with a rifle.

# CHAPTER THIRTYFIVE

Adam took a step towards Sam, staring him straight in the eyes, hoping he would stay calm and let him talk to him. "Sam, put the gun down man. You don't understand what is happening here, these people are trying to help us, not harm us."

"No Adam, you don't understand. I know exactly what's going on! Drugs! That's it, you are all on some new drug, and it's made everyone in this god forsaken city go crazy!"

Sam's voice quivered as he spoke, his volume rose, and then dropped, and it was obvious he wasn't in a fit state of mind. It was understandable; the death of another who is close to you can have a remarkable effect on a human being. Sam was the witness to his colleagues being killed earlier by the Denees, who at that stage believed they were just defending themselves from those who had hunted them for so many generations. But like anyone in grief, the reasons and plain laws of life that determine who will die, and who will live at any moment in time, they meant nothing to Sam. All one can do is feel the pain of who they have lost, and can't stop the yearning for what once was, and for changing what has happened, while at the same time knowing this just can't be, and Sam was no different from any other human being in this respect. The only real difference was that for Sam, not only had he witnessed the death of his friends and colleagues, but on top of that he had his World turned upside down like the rest of the citizens of Duntoon.

Eliza suddenly picked up the weapon that she and Charles earlier had used to control the group's first meeting with, she pointed it at Sam, and though he quickly swung his rifle in her direction, she fired a beam of energy at him that froze him on the spot for several seconds before he fell to the floor in an apparent lifeless body.

No one spoke, and instead they all sat or stood where they had been when Sam had entered the room, their eyes moving back and forth from Sam's body to Eliza.

Charles strode slowly over to Eliza, placed a hand on her shoulder and spoke quietly to her.

"It's ok my love, you did what needed to be done." He then took the weapon from her hand, and walked over to Sam, pointing the weapon at his body once more.

"No, Charles, please don't kill him. Or, or is he already dead?" Adam asked.

"He will be if I do not revive him within the next few minutes," Charles said as he bent down and took the rifle from Sam, looking at it as if it was a rare relic he had just found on an archaeological dig.

"I am gong to revive him now, but if he makes another aggressive move towards us, I will be forced to render him unconscious once more. How do you people know this man? Are we likely to come across more aggressive men like him if we are to stay with you in this city?"

"No, I think Sam is merely a victim of a traumatic experience," Trish answered, walking over to Sam to do what she did best - nurse him. "He saw his colleagues and friends killed only days ago, and I don't think it is something he is likely to get over soon at all. Especially when the one cure for his ailment is finding reason and understanding in what he experienced, and those two things are beyond the reach of any of us at the moment."

Charles pointed the weapon, come healing device at Sam's torso and pulled the trigger, a fine soft blue line of light shot from it, and within a few seconds Sam opened his eyes, and looked into Trish's face as she was now bent down beside him.

"You will feel weak for an hour or two young man," Charles advised him. "I don't want to see you move from that spot though. You can sit up, but other than that, don't move or I will be forced to incapacitate you again, and if you have to be woken from that state once more, it will be several hours before you fully recover."

Charles strode over to Richie, who he now seemed to trust wholeheartedly, and handed him the rifle that Sam held only minutes before.

"Guard him, my friend." Charles smiled like a father at Richie, patted him on the shoulder and joined his Wife by her side.

Eliza was now standing back at the device she had constructed, and with a smile, switched the simplistic switch to the on position. Despite the group expecting some sort of flash, or the deafening sound of thunder, all they experienced instead was the sight of a gentle glow come from the crystal that powered the contraption.

"Bummer, looks like a total fail," Larry said, with genuine disappointment in his voice.

"No, not a fail Larry, it is working as it is meant to - the force field will now be in effect in almost exactly the same place the purple shield was for those hundreds of years that you were trapped in time. The fact the crystal is glowing shows that the power is being generated and rerouted into an atmospheric arc, which will mushroom in shape and cover the city as we are wanting," Eliza reassured Larry, and the rest of the group.

"So, we are now safe from the elite and the rest of the Denees getting into the area?" Sam asked.

"We are, or at least for now anyway."

"For now?" Trish quipped, "You mean we won't be for long?"

"Well, this type of force field is effective, and is very similar to that used by the Elite cities to protect themselves. However, it is not impossible to decipher the key code, and neutralise the shield. This will take a lot of time, maybe as long as two or even three months, but it can be done. We will need to be on our guard, constantly, and when they decipher the code and neutralise the shield, we will need to immediately start another shield, which will need to be at least one hundred metres or so behind where the current one is. The distance is needed to be able to give it a different key code, which in turn will need to be deciphered before it can be neutralised."

"Why can't we simply set up several other force fields now, so we don't have to wait until the current one is, um, turned off by the Elite?" Adam asked.

"Adam, the technology behind these shields is very complex, and not so easy to explain to someone over 350 years behind in current scientific knowledge." Eliza smiled as she spoke, to give a feeling not of condescendence, but more of explanation. "Look at it like this, what would happen if you had, what I believe was once called an X-ray, but you received a blast of radiation that was ten thousand times what it should have been?"

"You would be fried big time man!" Larry quickly commented, waving his hand in the air like it had just been burnt.

"Yes, and that is what happens if you run more than one of these shields simultaneously. The energy combines, as it is attracted much like the pull of two magnets towards each other. The resulting energy would kill everything within a hundred kilometres. We can also not move the new shield forward when started up, as the new shield would have to pass over the resonance stored in the ground from the last shield, subsequently over time the area the shield protects will become smaller and smaller. Within several years time, we will need to move from here, or somehow protect ourselves without the use of force-fields."

Princess Amberley moved to a position where she was in front of the group, and now facing the group. They looked to her as people in a religious congregation would towards a Minister of faith, even though the native Duntoon residents still hardly knew her, let alone understood exactly what she represented. Yet there was something about her that just seemed to make them feel at ease and at peace, even in these unprecedented circumstances.

We need to come together as one people. There is now a new people, not Elites, nor Denees, but New Duntoonians, and we shall call this area New Duntoon. Together we can face the challenges the future will present. Working as one we can overcome the challenges of food supplies, of coming to terms with our different backgrounds, and with defending ourselves from the enemies that now lay mostly on the other side of the shield that Eliza has provided us with. But most importantly, let us all learn from what has occurred over the last 350 years. Let us not be fooled by any man or group who wishes to use fear of something that is not real, but who tries to assure us it is, all in the name of wealth. Let common sense and the camaraderie of togetherness and moving towards the same goals protect us from such stupidity for the rest of time." The Princess's voice had remained as quiet and calm during her speech as they had heard it before, yet it was full of confidence and authority that seemed to quell any remaining feeling of unease amongst the group of the new citizens of New Duntoon.

Adam reached out and held his Wife's hand. "Trish, it will be alright. I love you."

Trish smiled at Adam, kissed him on the cheek and told him "I love you too Adam. Yes, yes I think everything will be alright. There are a lot of things that will be coming our way that we have never faced before, but as long as we are together with our new friends, we can face them all."

**COMING IN MID 2012**


**BOOK TWO OF THE SAGA 'A DARK NIGHT A
LONG NIGHT'**


**'To Enter A City'**

**By Trevor Lewis**